MARGUERITE BENNETT

ARIELA KRISTANTINA

INSEXts

VOLUME

2

THE NECROPOLIS

JESSICA KHOLINNE

A LARGER WORLD

AFTERSHOCK

IN

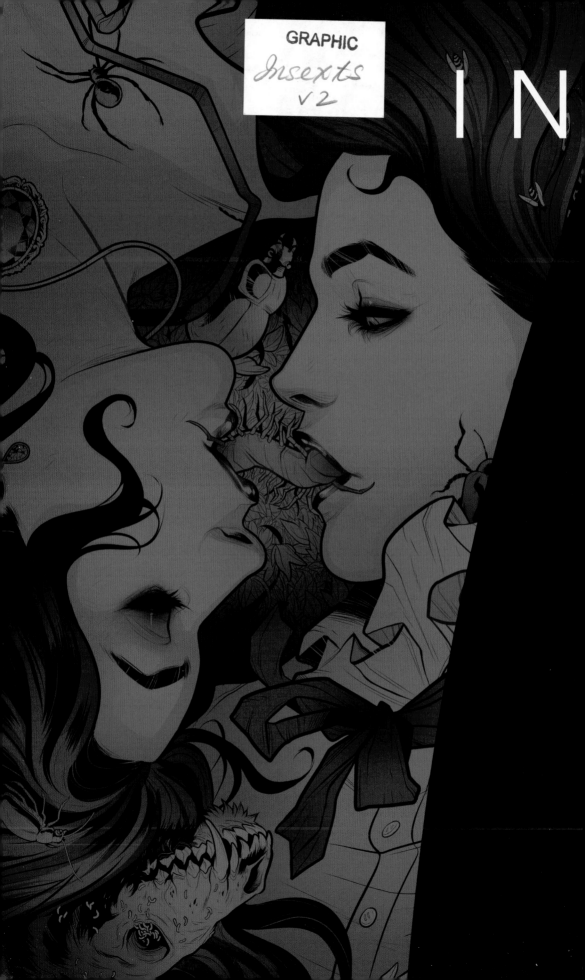

SEXTS

VOLUME 2
THE NECROPOLIS

MARGUERITE BENNETT creator & writer

ARIELA KRISTANTINA artist

JESSICA KHOLINNE colorist

A LARGER WORLD'S TROY PETERI letterer

ARIELA KRISTANTINA w/ **JESSICA KHOLINNE** front & original series covers

ELIZABETH TORQUE variant cover

JOHN J. HILL book & logo designer

MIKE MARTS editor

AFTERSHOCK™

MIKE MARTS - Editor-in-Chief • JOE PRUETT - Publisher/ Chief Creative Officer • LEE KRAMER - President
JAWAD QURESHI - SVP, Investor Relations • JON KRAMER - Chief Executive Officer • MIKE ZAGARI - SVP, Brand
JAY BEHLING - Chief Financial Officer • STEPHAN NILSON - Publishing Operations Manager
LISA Y. WU - Retailer/Fan Relations Manager • ASHLEY WYATT - Publishing Assistant

AfterShock Trade Dress and Interior Design by JOHN J. HILL • AfterShock Logo Design by COMICRAFT
Original series production by CHARLES PRITCHETT • Proofreading by DOCTOR Z.
Publicity: contact AARON MARION (aaron@fifteenminutes.com) &
RYAN CROY (ryan@fifteenminutes.com) at 15 MINUTES
Special thanks to TEDDY LEO & LISA MOODY

AFTERSHOCKCOMICS.COM   Follow us on social media 🐦 📷 f

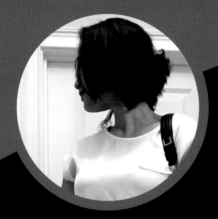

INTRODUCTION

"Would you be interested in drawing two ladies who can turn into insects and chase bad guys in Victorian Era Europe?"

I'm paraphrasing a bit, but that was the sales pitch I heard from my editor Mike Marts two short years ago. He added in that Marguerite Bennett was writing the story. With a pitch like that, who could in their right mind say "no"? I set aside my fear of looking at—let alone studying or drawing—insects, and said, "hell yes." Little did I expect how tender, sensual, emotional, intense, ingenious, violent and powerful the story was going to be! Marguerite really challenged me to raise my standards every issue. I love drawing backgrounds and environments...breathing life to INSEXTS using the world the characters occupy gives me so much joy. I want to take the readers on this amazing journey to the (un)known world of Lady, Mariah and Little Will.

Working with a great team is truly a privilege. Bryan Valenza and Jessica Kholinne were both superb colorists with their own unique visions and styles. They were never back-up singers, but instead were lead guitarists who filled each gap on my page, improved every line, and, most importantly, told the tale in a way I couldn't achieve alone. Additionally, A Larger World's lettering proved to efficiently support every scene change smoothly.

Last but not least, it's you, the readers, who matter the most. I couldn't be happier receiving such huge amounts of love, support and acceptance from all of you for INSEXTS. Each reader is important to me, and I'm glad you've all been able to share in such a unique journey with Lady, Mariah and Little Will.

Thank you.
ARIELA KRISTANTINA

8

"BELLE ÉPOQUE"

Père Lachaise Cemetery.
Paris. 1897.
SCRAAAAPE
SCRAAAAPE
THUD
THUNK
HAHA.
SQUELCH POP
HEH
HEH.
WSSSSSHH
EH?

WHO'S LURKIN' THERE?
YE SHOW YESELF, ELSE I'LL BURY YE HERE WITH THESE BLOATERS--
!
THUNK
!
HEH. JES' STONE.
?

SCHLPLECK
BLOSSSH
GSSSSH
DO NOT RUN, MY BEAUTY...
...I SHALL NOT KILL THEE.

AAAAH!
PANT PANT
AAAH!
SQUELCH
AAAHHH!
LET ME GO! LET ME GO!
FOR THE LOVE OF GOD, I--I DON'T WANT TO DIE!

THOU SHALT NOT DIE, BEAUTY...
...OH, NO...
...THOU SHALT LIVE...
...FOREVER.

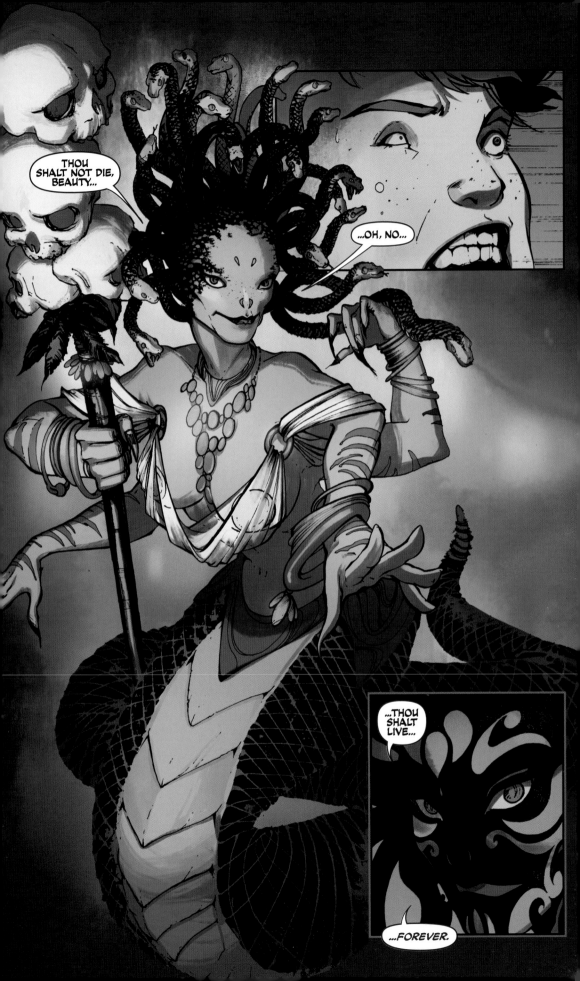

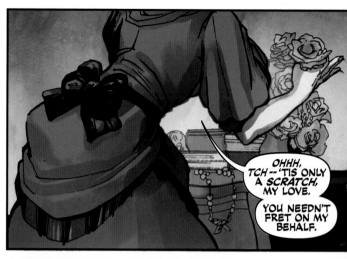

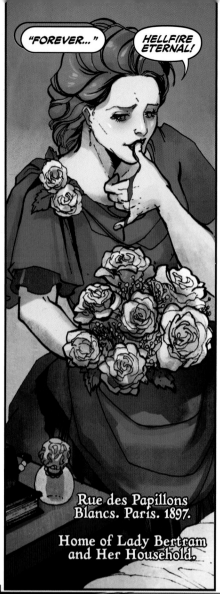

"FOREVER..." HELLFIRE ETERNAL!

Rue des Papillons Blancs. Paris. 1897.

Home of Lady Bertram and Her Household.

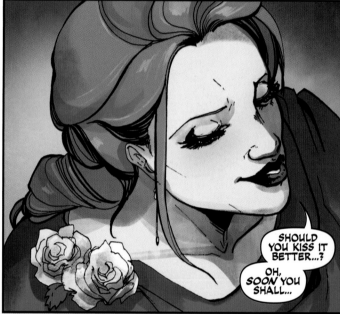

OHHH, TCH -- 'TIS ONLY A SCRATCH, MY LOVE.

YOU NEEDN'T FRET ON MY BEHALF.

SHOULD YOU KISS IT BETTER...? OH, SOON YOU SHALL...

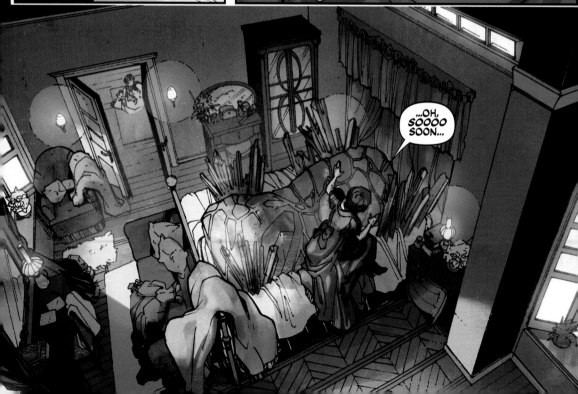

...OH, SOOOO SOON...

YOUR MOTHER WILL BE AWAKE SOON, MY WILL!
IN TIME FOR MY *BIRTHDAY*, MAMA?
IN TIME FOR *MANY THINGS*, MY HEART.
SHE HAS SLEPT LONG AND WELL SINCE OUR LITTLE ENGLISH ENDEAVORS.
WE MUST HAVE EVERYTHING IN READINESS FOR WHEN SHE WAKES.
ARE YOU READY TO MEET YOUR *NEW GOVERNESS?*
YES, MAMA!
NOK NOK!
AH, THE BELLMAN MUST'VE LET HER UP...
HELLO, MADEMOISELLE PHOEBE DE AZAÏS.

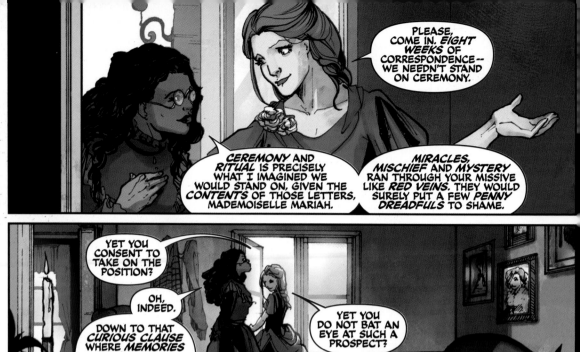

PLEASE, COME IN. *EIGHT WEEKS* OF CORRESPONDENCE-- WE NEEDN'T STAND ON CEREMONY.

CEREMONY AND *RITUAL* IS PRECISELY WHAT I IMAGINED WE WOULD STAND ON, GIVEN THE *CONTENTS* OF THOSE LETTERS, MADEMOISELLE MARIAH.

MIRACLES, MISCHIEF AND *MYSTERY* RAN THROUGH YOUR MISSIVE LIKE *RED VEINS.* THEY WOULD SURELY PUT A FEW *PENNY DREADFULS* TO SHAME.

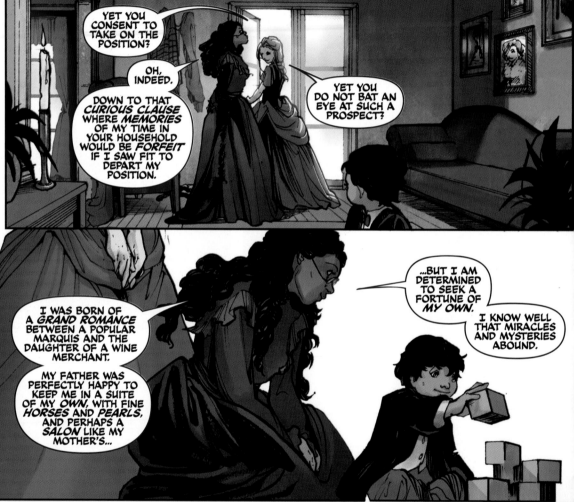

YET YOU CONSENT TO TAKE ON THE POSITION?

OH, INDEED.

DOWN TO THAT *CURIOUS CLAUSE* WHERE *MEMORIES* OF MY TIME IN YOUR HOUSEHOLD WOULD BE *FORFEIT* IF I SAW FIT TO DEPART MY POSITION.

YET YOU DO NOT BAT AN EYE AT SUCH A PROSPECT?

...BUT I AM DETERMINED TO SEEK A FORTUNE OF *MY OWN.*

I KNOW WELL THAT MIRACLES AND MYSTERIES ABOUND.

I WAS BORN OF A *GRAND ROMANCE* BETWEEN A POPULAR MARQUIS AND THE DAUGHTER OF A WINE MERCHANT.

MY FATHER WAS PERFECTLY HAPPY TO KEEP ME IN A SUITE OF MY *OWN*, WITH FINE *HORSES* AND *PEARLS*, AND PERHAPS A *SALON* LIKE MY MOTHER'S...

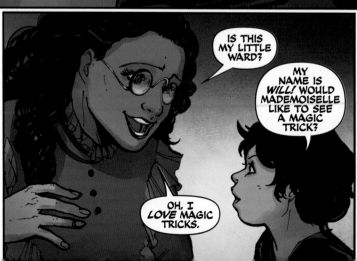

IS THIS MY LITTLE WARD?

MY NAME IS *WILL!* WOULD MADEMOISELLE LIKE TO SEE A MAGIC TRICK?

OH, I *LOVE* MAGIC TRICKS.

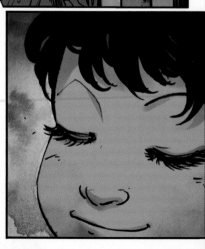

!
IF YOU CHOSE TO REMAIN WITH US, PHOEBE, YOUR ROLE WOULD BE *FAR* MORE THAN THAT OF *GOVERNESS.*
YOU WOULD OPERATE AS BUTLER AND HOUSEKEEPER.
YOU WOULD DELIVER MESSAGES FOR US.
YOU WOULD LIVE HERE, AND KEEP OUR SECRETS.
I HAVE KEPT SECRETS *MY LIFE LONG.*
IT WOULD BE A *DELIGHT* TO FINALLY SHARE THEM WITH THOSE WHO HAVE SECRETS IN TURN.
IT HAS BEEN MANY YEARS OF WINTERS, PHOEBE.
I HOPE THIS IS THE BEGINNING OF *SPRING*, AND THE RETURN OF THE *SUN.*
MAMA! HOW *SOON* WILL MOTHER BE JOINING?
SO SOON, MY SWEET... PLAY BUT A MOMENT...

I SHALL HAVE YOUR ROOM HERE IN READINESS FOR WHEN YOU RETURN, PHOEBE.
THE HOUSE IS STILL BEING PREPARED -- THE GARDEN IS A RUIN, AND WE HAVEN'T EVEN A STATUE ON THE OLD FOUNTAIN --
QUICK. THE WITCH IS LEAVING --
!
PHOEBE!
GET INSIDE, THEY MUST'VE FOLLOWED MY LADY FROM LONDON, THEY --
...WE AREN'T HERE FOR *YOU*, YOU LITTLE STRAWBERRY TART...
...WE'RE HERE FOR *THE HARUSPEX.*
IS *THAT* WHAT YOU THINK I DO?
CARVE OPEN GUTS WITH MY PAINTER'S PALETTE, ALL TO TELL THE FUTURE?
GO BACK TO YOUR *GALLERIES* AND *MUSEUMS*, MONSIEUR ROQUÉPINE--
--I'D HATE TO SHOW WHAT *YOUR* FUTURE HOLDS.

YOU'LL *DIE* FOR WHAT YOU'VE DONE, WITCH--!
KRAK
SHHHHH...
NO...*NO*, I DON'T WANT TO--
NO!
AAAAAH!
RUN!
I--WHERE ARE WE?
WHO WAS--WHAT WERE WE DOING HERE, *HOW*--?

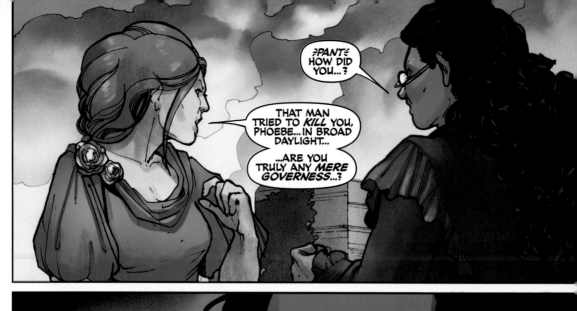

≀PANT≀
HOW DID YOU...?

THAT MAN TRIED TO *KILL* YOU, PHOEBE...IN BROAD DAYLIGHT...

...ARE YOU TRULY ANY *MERE* GOVERNESS...?

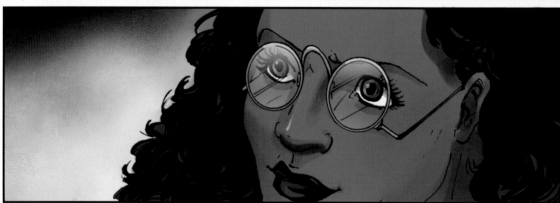

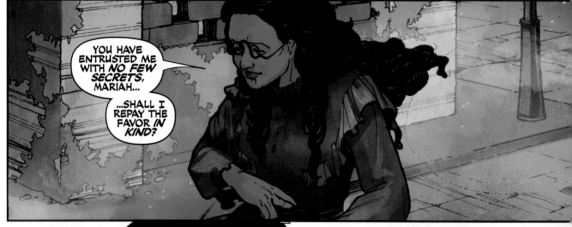

YOU HAVE ENTRUSTED ME WITH *NO FEW SECRETS,* MARIAH...

...SHALL I REPAY THE FAVOR *IN KIND?*

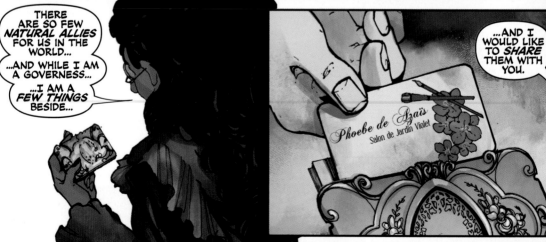

THERE ARE SO FEW *NATURAL ALLIES* FOR US IN THE WORLD...

...AND WHILE I AM A GOVERNESS...

...I AM A *FEW THINGS* BESIDE...

...AND I WOULD LIKE TO *SHARE* THEM WITH YOU.

Phoebe de Azaïs
Salon de Jardin Violet

Rue des Papillons Blancs. Night.
"PYGMALION WAS A SCULPTOR, AND CARVED OF IVORY A SNOW-WHITE GIRL, PERFECT IN HIS EYES AND PRISTINE IN HIS HEART..."
...HE LOVED THE STATUE MORE THAN ANY LIVING WOMAN, AND PRAYED TO APHRODITE, GODDESS OF LOVE, TO MAKE HER AS REAL AS YOU OR I...
"...DO YOU LIKE THIS STORY, WILL?"
"NO, MAMÁ."
"NOR DO I, MY HEART, NOW THAT I READ IT AGAIN..."
MAY I HAVE A BETTER STORY FOR MY BIRTHDAY?
"OH, YES, MY DARLING..."

"...I HAVE A FAR BETTER BIRTHDAY PRESENT IN MIND."
YOU TRIED TO KILL A GIRL TODAY, MONSIEUR... ROQUÉPINE, WAS IT?
UNNATURAL
UNNATURAL WOMEN
RUINING
RUINING
UN UN UN UN NATURAL
IS THAT ALL YOU HAVE TO SAY?
PERHAPS THE TIP OF YOUR KNIFE CLIPPED THE FRONT OF YOUR BRAIN.
KILL HER KILL HARU
KILL HER FOR WHAT SHE IS WHAT SHE DID
WELL, IN THAT CASE...
...SHHHHHH...
HRRR-!
SQUOLCH
♬♪FROM ROT THE BEAUTIES OF THE WORLD CAN ONLY EVER SPRING♬♪

...WAKE, MY LIFE...
CHITTER CHITTER CHITTER
BZZZZ
WAKE, MY LOVE...
FLUTTER FLUTTER
...WAKE...
HSSSSS
...WAKE...
CHITTER CHITTER CHITTER
...MY LADY...
KSSSSHH

OH, MY MARIAH...
...I HAVE MISSED YOU.

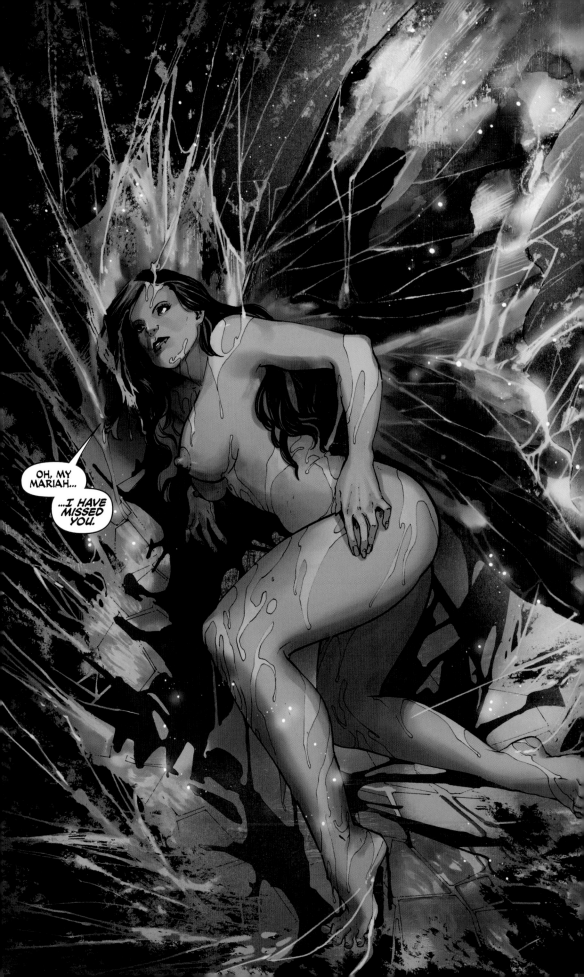

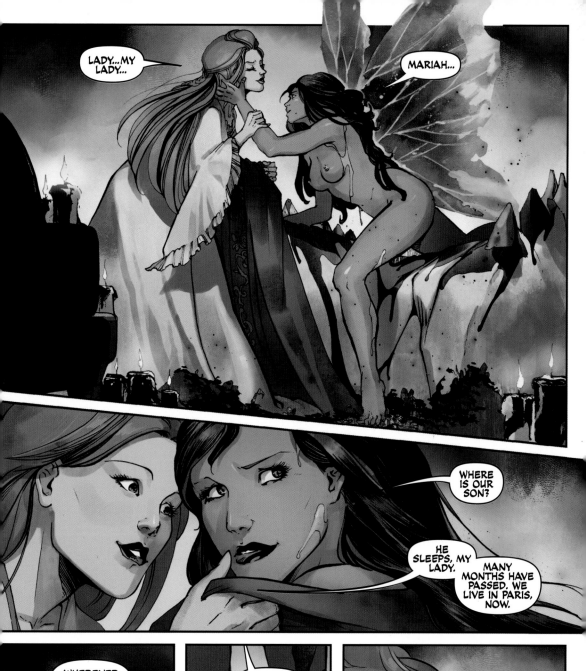

LADY...MY LADY...

MARIAH...

WHERE IS OUR SON?

HE SLEEPS, MY LADY. MANY MONTHS HAVE PASSED. WE LIVE IN PARIS, NOW.

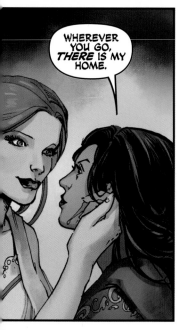

WHEREVER YOU GO, *THERE* IS MY HOME.

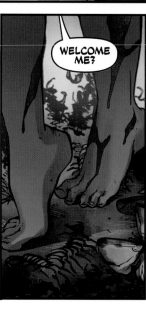

WELCOME ME?

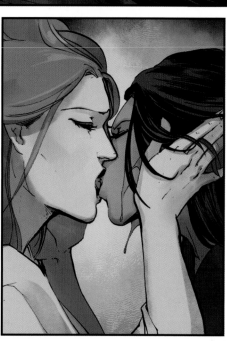

"WELCOME HOME."

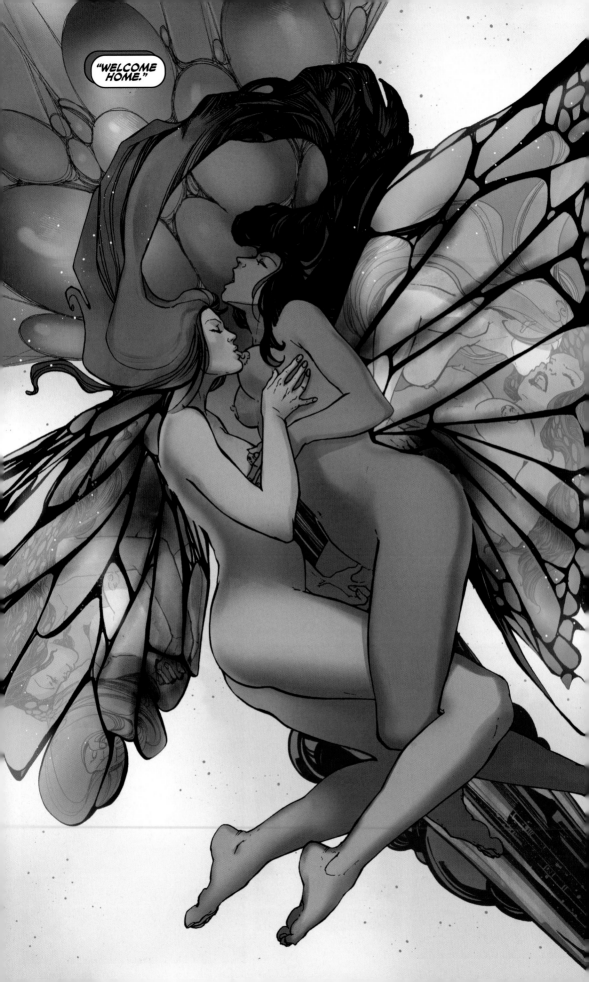

HOW DID YOU KNOW WHEN TO WAKE ME? HOW DID YOU KNOW HOW?
I KNEW AS SURELY AS BIRDS KNOW HOW TO FLY, MY LADY...AND WHERE TO GO, AND NEST IN WINTER...
WITH NEW JOYS...
OH, OUR SON...! HE HAS GROWN SO...!
...WE ARE NEW CREATURES, WITH NEW INSTINCTS, IT WOULD SEEM...
MY LADY...
...THERE IS SOMEONE IN THE GARDEN.
THE MAN I USED TO REVIVE YOU HAD COMRADES, BUT I THOUGHT I HAD BEWITCHED THEM TO FORGET WHERE THEY WERE WHEN HE FELL.
SURELY THEY DID NOT THINK TO--
OH...
...OH, MY...
PERHAPS MY RESURRECTION IS BUT ANOTHER BIRTHDAY, MY LOVE...

...FOR SOMEONE HAS BROUGHT US A *GIFT*.
NEXT:
INSEXTS
CHAPTER IX

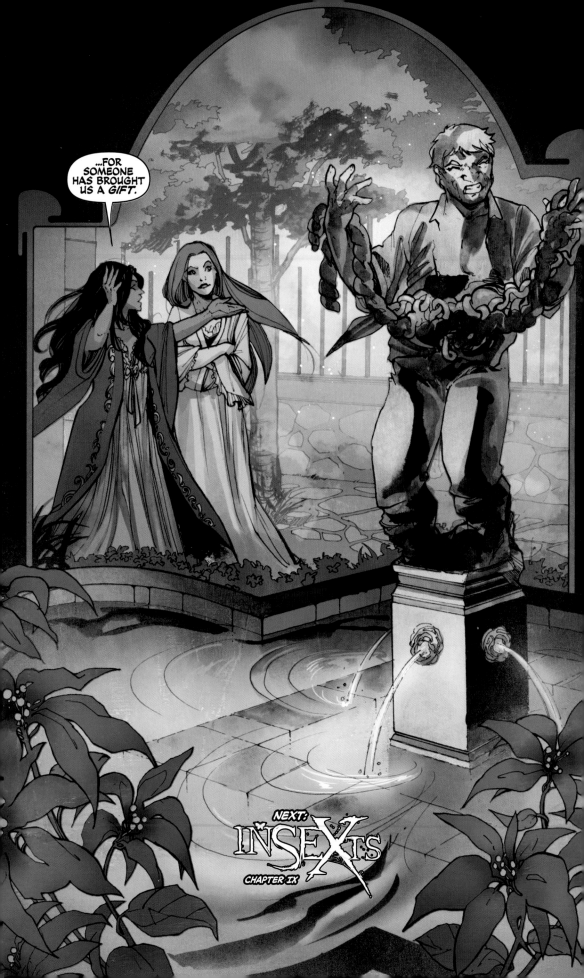

9

"PRETTY PICTURES"

PERFECT.
PALE AND PURE AND PERFECT.
SILENT. STILL. BEAUTIFUL.
SEEN AND NEVER HEARD.
TENDER, WILTING--
--CHASTE.
PERSEPHONE, QUEEN OF THE UNDERWORLD...

Le Musée Silencieux. Paris. 1897.
...THE PERFECT WOMAN.
WHAT ELSE COULD COMPARE...?
THE GRACES, PERHAPS...

...A HAREM OF PERFECTION AND--
AHH!
SILENT...?
STILL...?
SEEN AND NEVER HEARD...
CRK
TENDER, WILTING...
...CHASED.

DO NOT RUN...
...I SHALL NOT *KILL* THEE...
WHKK
...INDEED, I SHALL GIVE THEE WHAT THOU DESIREST...
...I SHALL GIVE THEE...
...THE PERFECT WOMAN.

PLEASE-- PLEASE, NO!
I ONLY-- I ONLY WATCHED, TOUCHED, I DID NOT--I WAS NOT THE ONE WHO--
--PLEASE...?
ER-PERSEPHONE?
...
MY LOVE.

!
NFF! NHHFFF!

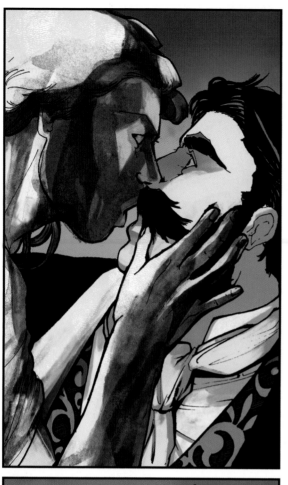

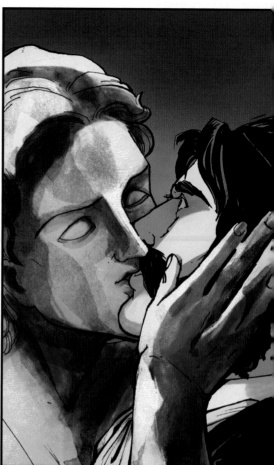

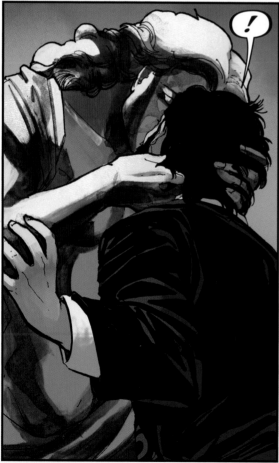

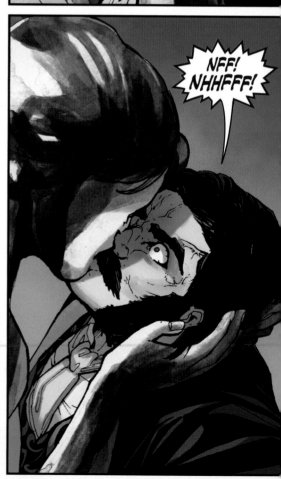

CRK
SQUORCH
LOVELY, MY DARLING...
...WHAT A PRETTY PICTURE THOU HAST MADE.

Le Jardin Des Violets. Paris.
THE PRETTIEST PICTURES INDEED, MY DOVE! PRETTY AS YOUR PRETTY NEW GOVERNESS, PRETTY AS ALL YOUR TOY HORSES--
--PRETTY AS THE GIFT OF THAT STONE STATUE THAT GRACES OUR FOUNTAIN, HOLDING HIS GUTS OUT LIKE GIFTS ON THE ALTAR.
MY LADY, THE MEN WHO MEANT YOUNG PHOEBE ILL, WHO ATTACKED HER OUTSIDE OF OUR TOWNHOUSE...
...DO YOU THINK IT WAS THEY WHO LEFT THE GIFT OF THAT STRANGE STATUE? A WARNING?
OR PHOEBE HERSELF...?
I THINK IT ONLY FAIR TO ASK, THAT WE MAY RENDER OUR VARYING THANKS IN PERSON.
TELL ME, MY WILL...DOES IT FEEL SAFE TO ENTER?
YES, MOTHER.
OUR FRIENDS ARE INSIDE.
MY CLEVER BOY.
MY LITTLE PRINCE...

...LET US GO AND MEET THEM.

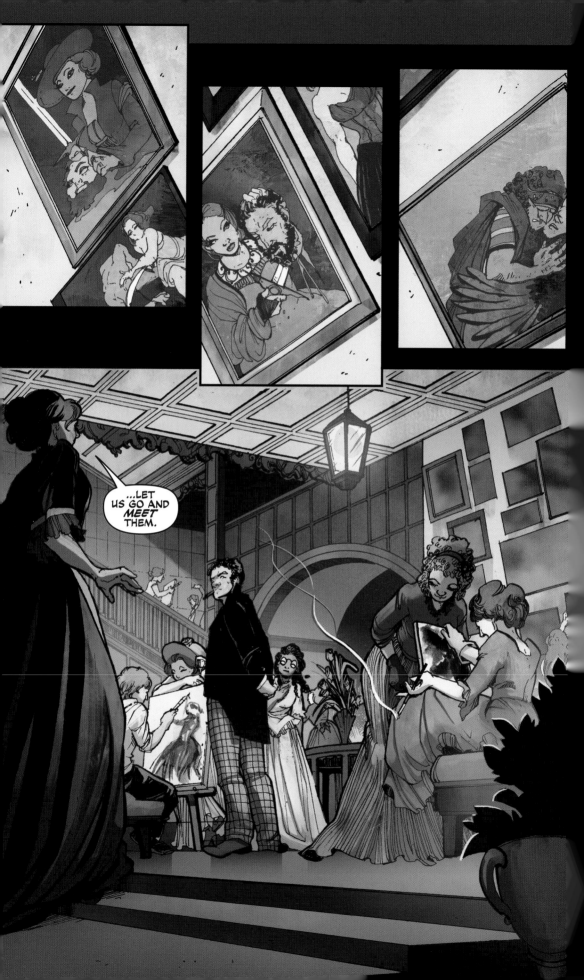

MARIAH!
I AM SO GLAD YOU HAVE COME--
PHOEBE!
YOU ALREADY KNOW MAMA, BUT WOULD YOU LIKE TO MEET MOTHER?
LADY, A PLEASURE AT LAST!
PLEASE PERMIT ME TO INTRODUCE MY OWN MOTHER, DOROTHÉE DE AZAÏS, THE MISTRESS OF THIS SALON.
WE ARE NONE OF US PERMITTED ENTRANCE INTO THE GRAND ACADEMIES OF THE ARTS, ANY MORE THAN OUR ART IS WELCOME IN THE GREAT MUSEUMS.
INSTEAD, MY PUPILS COME TO LEARN AND EXHIBIT HERE.
MY MOTHER IS AN EXQUISITE SCULPTOR. ONE OF THE REASONS MY FATHER FELL IN LOVE WITH HER--
--TO HIM, SHE CREATED LIFE LONG BEFORE SHE BORE HIS CHILD.
AND MY DAUGHTER HAS BEEN SEEKING YOU FOR A LONG TIME, MADAME ET MADEMOISELLE.
SHE BELIEVES YOU CAN HUNT THE ONES HUNTING US.
PHOEBE?

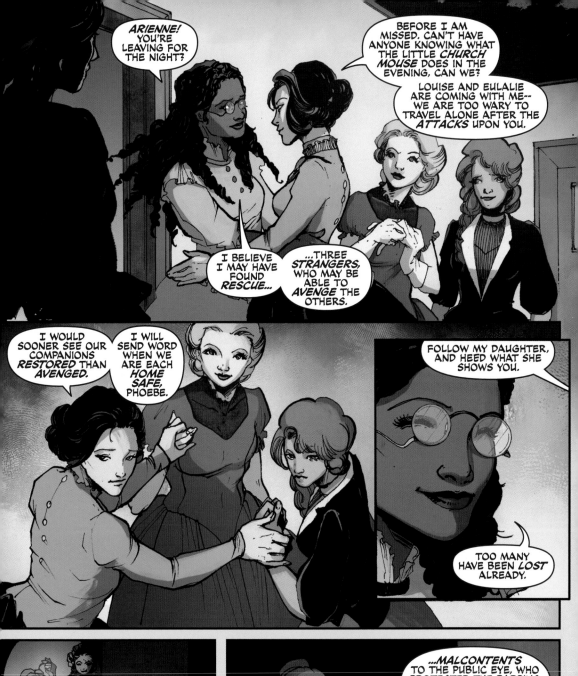

ARIENNE! YOU'RE LEAVING FOR THE NIGHT?

BEFORE I AM MISSED. CAN'T HAVE ANYONE KNOWING WHAT THE LITTLE *CHURCH MOUSE* DOES IN THE EVENING, CAN WE?

LOUISE AND EULALIE ARE COMING WITH ME-- WE ARE TOO WARY TO TRAVEL ALONE AFTER THE *ATTACKS* UPON YOU.

I BELIEVE I MAY HAVE FOUND *RESCUE*...

...THREE *STRANGERS*, WHO MAY BE ABLE TO *AVENGE* THE OTHERS.

I WOULD SOONER SEE OUR COMPANIONS *RESTORED* THAN AVENGED.

I WILL SEND WORD WHEN WE ARE EACH *HOME SAFE*, PHOEBE.

FOLLOW MY DAUGHTER, AND HEED WHAT SHE SHOWS YOU.

TOO MANY HAVE BEEN *LOST* ALREADY.

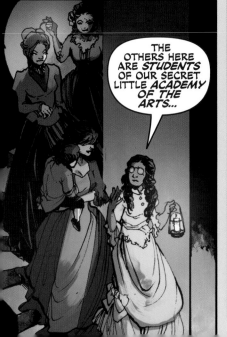

THE OTHERS HERE ARE *STUDENTS* OF OUR SECRET LITTLE *ACADEMY OF THE ARTS*...

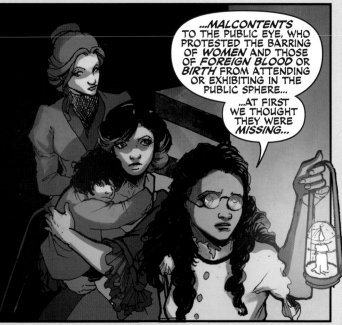

...*MALCONTENTS* TO THE PUBLIC EYE, WHO PROTESTED THE BARRING OF *WOMEN* AND THOSE OF *FOREIGN BLOOD* OR *BIRTH* FROM ATTENDING OR EXHIBITING IN THE PUBLIC SPHERE...

...AT FIRST WE THOUGHT THEY WERE *MISSING*...

...BUT THEN WE *FOUND* THEM.
I DO NOT UNDERSTAND...
...THESE ARE PAINTINGS *OF* OR *BY* THE *MISSING PUPILS?*
...BUT THESE *ARE* THE MISSING PUPILS.
FORGIVE MY THEATRICS, MY LADY...
"...*CAPTURED* THEIR IMAGE.

AFTER THEY VANISHED, *RENEGADE STUDENTS* OF OUR ACADEMY FOUND THESE WAITING TO BE SHOW-CASED AT MSSR. RODERICK'S *MUSÉE SILENCIEUX.*
HE HAS, SHALL WE SAY...
"WE WOULD SNEAK THEIR ART INTO GALLERIES, *DISGUISE* OURSELVES AS YOUNG MEN TO ATTEND THEIR CLASSES, PASS OUT PAMPHLETS DECRYING THE BARRING OF OUR RANKS FROM THE WORLD OF HIGH ART--
"EACH WOMAN *PROVOKED* THAT COUNCIL OF *THWARTED ARTISTS* AND *CONDESCENDING CURATORS.*
"--SHOW OURSELVES AS *UNWOMANLY WOMEN.*
"PROVE OURSELVES..."

"...UNNATURAL."
MAMA--
--MOTHER!

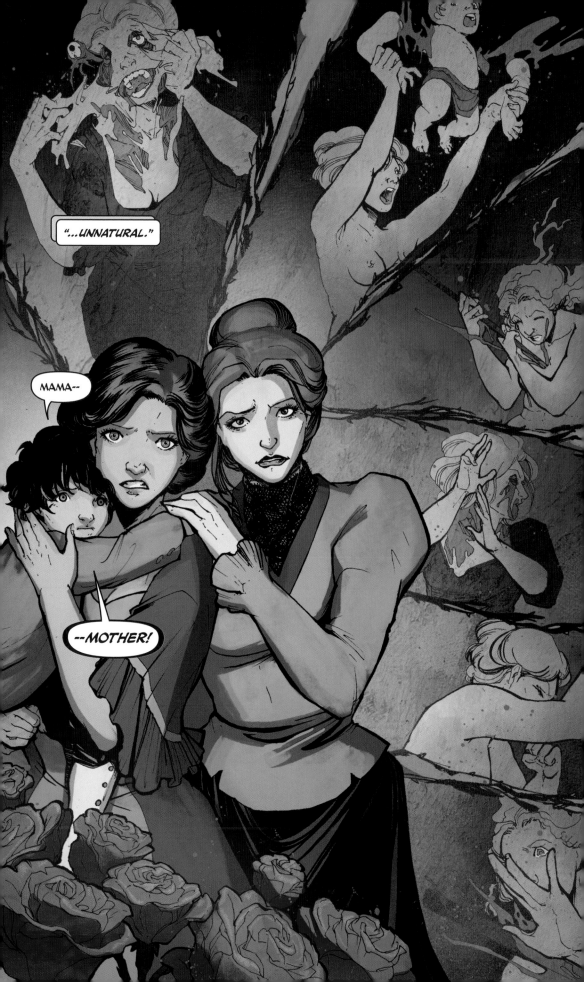

YOU SEE THE DARK MYSTERY WE FACE, *MADAME ET MADEMOISELLE*...
...WE ARE BEING STALKED, HUNTED, *TRANSFORMED* BY THESE WRETCHED OLD GATEKEEPERS...
M-MOTHER?
...WE MUST FIND A WAY TO *UNDO* WHAT HAS BEEN *DONE* TO OUR SISTERS.
WE MUST STOP THE ONES WHO HAVE *IMPRISONED* THEM...

"...AND WE DO NOT HAVE THE POWER TO *DEFEND THEM ALL.*"
WHAT A *REMARKABLE* SHOWING! DID YOU SEE MADAME'S SCULPTURE OF *ARTEMIS AND ACTAEON?*
EVERYONE ELSE DEPICTS ARTEMIS *NAKED* AND *BATHING* WHILE ACTAEON LEERS FROM THE BUSHES, BUT MADAME'S STATUE HAD THE HOUNDS TEARING ACTAEON LIMB FROM LIMB WHILE ARTEMIS DREW HER BOW TO--
ARIENNE ZHANG...?
WARD OF THE *ÉGLISE DE SAINTE-ADÉLAÏDE?*
THERE'S A PRICE FOR WOMEN WHO ASK FOR *TROUBLE,* YOU LITTLE WITCH...
BILL ME.
BLAM
YOU THINK WE'LL GO *QUIETLY?!* YOU THINK YOU'LL PUT ALL THE WOMEN IN THE WORLD BACK INTO A *CELL?!*
NOT INTO A *CELL,* MADEMOISELLE...

"...INTO A PRETTY, PRETTY PICTURE."
...
?
!!
LOUISE! EULALIE!
WHERE-- WHERE ARE WE?!
WHERE--?!

YOU'RE EXACTLY WHERE YOU BELONG, ARIENNE ZHANG.
ARIENNE, WHO INSULTED LE MUSÉE SILENCIEUX, AND ENCOURAGED A BOYCOTT OF ALL THE STUDENTS IN PARIS AGAINST ITS GREAT NAME.
WE ARE GOING TO EASE YOUR TROUBLED MIND--
I'LL SMEAR YOUR TROUBLED MIND ALL ALONG A SHITHOUSE BRICK, MSSR. RODERICK--
WE ARE GOING TO HELP YOU SERVE YOUR TRUE PURPOSE.
PUT AN END TO ALL THIS OUTRAGE.
A-ARIENNE--?!

fFFP
fP
HSSS
AT LAST...
...THEY ARE AS THEY SHOULD BE.

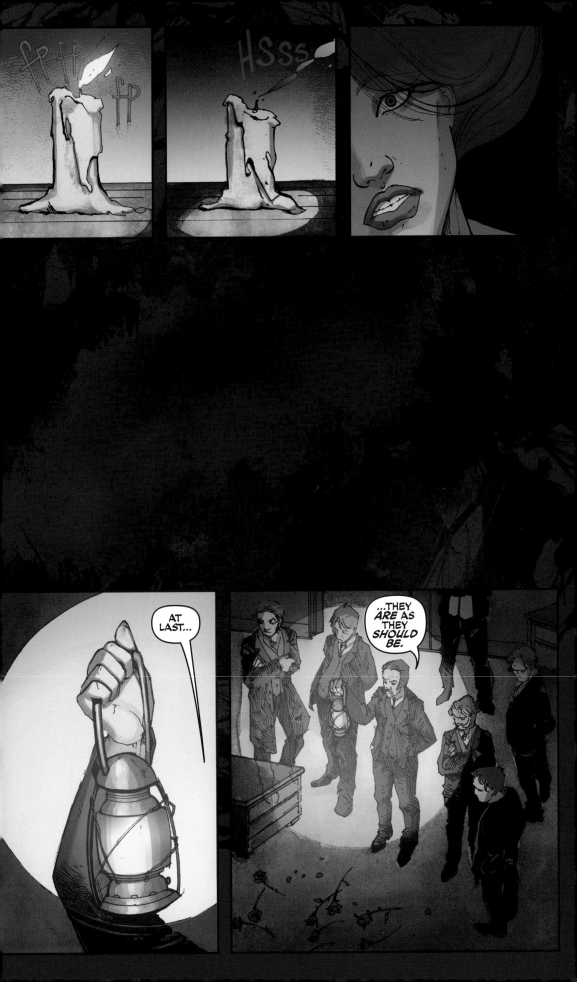

SILENT. CHASTE.
PERFECT.
NEXT:
INSEXTS
CHAPTER X

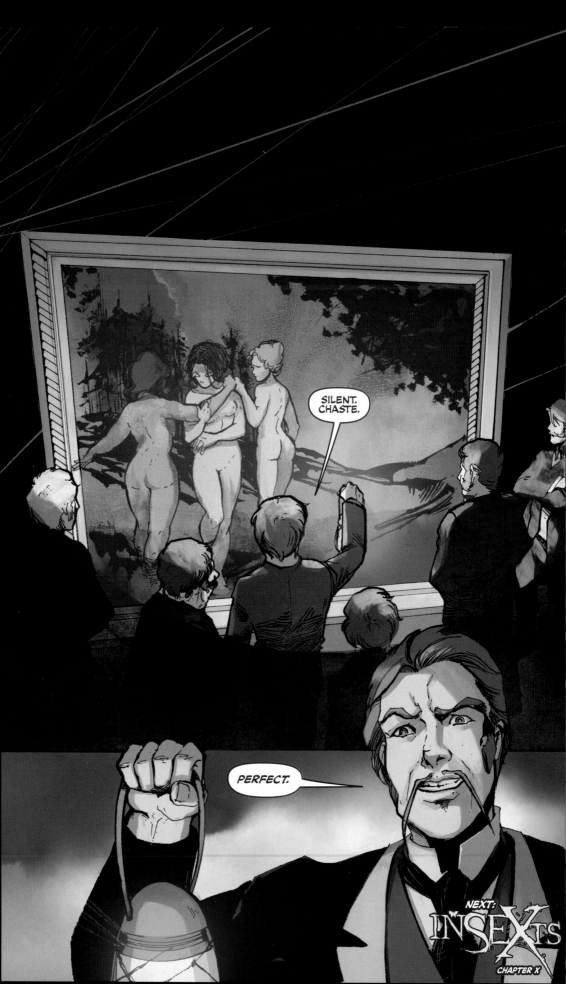

"NECROPOLIS"

10

OSSEMENT S-04
CIMETIÈRE DES
INNOCENTS
DÉPOSÉS LE 2 JUILLET 1896

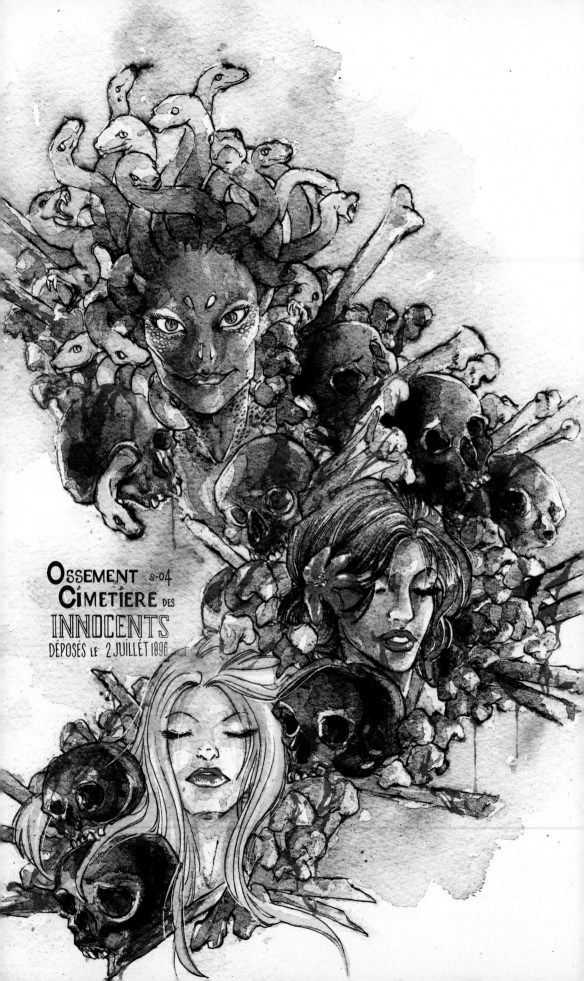

OSSEMENT s-04
CIMETIERE DES
INNOCENTS
DÉPOSÉS LE 2 JUILLÉT 1896

Le Musée Silencieux.
Paris. 1897.
A NEW WORK? YET THE CURATOR HAS GONE MISSING--
BUT THE ARTIST IS THE TRUE MASTER.
YES, RODERICK KNOWS HOW TO APPRECIATE THE FEMALE FORM.
BEAUTIFUL.
CLASSICAL.
CLEAN.
SILENT.
ELEGANT.
PERFECT.

HE GOT THEM. RODERICK GOT THEM.
EULALIE, LOUISE AND ARIENNE--MY MOTHER'S STUDENTS, MY FRIENDS--!
I WAS ONCE MADE THE ORNAMENT OF A VIOLENT MAN.
RODERICK WILL HOLD HIS GUTS IN HIS HANDS BEFORE HE DIES.
HE WILL POP HIS OWN EYES BETWEEN HIS TEETH AND FEEL THE JELLY RUN, SALT-SWEET, DOWN HIS THROAT.
THIS ARTIST WILL DECORATE MY SKIN AS GRISTLE AND SMEAR--
MADAME!

YOU MUST NOT TOUCH THE NEW ACQUISITION.
AHHH, HARUSPEX.
YOU HAVE SOME NERVE, BRINGING SUCH INDECENCIES INTO THIS PLACE. WE TOOK THREE GRACES TO REPLACE THE THREE YOU STOLE.
OR ARE THESE GIFTS TO BUY OUR MERCY? SHALL WE HANG THEM IN THE HALLS?
THIS ONE A HINDU QUEEN, LASCIVIOUS AND HONEY-SWEET.
THIS ONE THE LONG-SUFFERING IRISH MARTYR--PERHAPS ST. DYMPHNA, AT THE HOUR OF HER--
YOU KNOW YOU COULD RETURN TO US, MADEMOISELLE.
THE CRUCIAL MISUNDERSTANDING, MSSR., IS THAT I WAS EVER ONE OF YOU TO BEGIN WITH.

THE ACCLAIMED MSSR. RODERICK.
PERHAPS I MIGHT INTEREST YOU IN A NEW ACQUISITION OF MY OWN?
THERE IS A STATUE IN MY GARDEN THAT MIGHT BE QUITE TO YOUR... TASTES.
WITH RESPECT, I VERY MUCH DOUBT MADAME CAPABLE OF PRODUCING ART OF THE CALIBER IN WHICH THE MUSEUM WOULD BE INTERESTED.
WE DO NOT DISCRIMINATE, YOU SEE--WE MUST SIMPLY TAKE WHAT ART IS TRULY SUPERIOR.
YOU VALUE WOMEN OF INK AND PAINT OVER WOMEN OF FLESH AND BONE.
WOMEN OF INK AND PAINT RARELY CAUSE AS MUCH TROUBLE.
IT WAS YOUR SEX THAT RUINED FEMININITY, NOT OURS.
EVEN IF SUCH A NEBULOUS THING COULD EVER BE "RUINED", IT WOULD BE BY THE MEN WHO DECIDED FEMININITY WAS THEIRS TO DEFINE.
OUR PERSONHOOD, YOU MEAN.
DANTE ADORED HIS BEATRICE BECAUSE HE NEVER SPOKE TO HER, NOT ONCE, IN HIS ENTIRE LIFE. SHE WAS HIS TO NARRATE, MANIPULATE, PERFECT.
WOULD HIS PASSION HAVE BEEN SO ENDURING IF HE HAD EVER HEARD HER EXPRESS A SINGLE THOUGHT OF HER OWN?

WHEN HAS ANYTHING NOT BEEN A MAN'S TO DEFINE?
WE BUILT ALL OF CIVILIZATION, WHILE YOU SIT WITHIN ITS COMFORTS TO CLUCK AND COMPLAIN.
AND WHEN WE CREATE WONDERS, ODES TO YOUR PERFECTION, YOU SCORN US.
YOU DO NOT SING HYMNS TO OUR PERFECTION, MSSR.
YOU SING TO DROWN US OUT, AND PRAISE SOME FALSE IDOL WITH OUR NAMES.
YOU INVENT A FANTASY AND CONDEMN OUR FAILURE TO LIVE UP TO IT.
IS OUR FANTASY SUCH AN AFFRONT TO YOUR INSECURITY?
IT IS WHEN YOU RANK IT ABOVE OUR HUMANITY.
IT IS WHEN YOU DO NOT ACCORD US THE SAME RIGHT TO FANTASY-- OR, EVEN, THE RIGHT TO DEPICT THE TRUTH OF OUR OWN LIVES AT ALL.
WOMEN ARE ONLY PERMITTED ENTRANCE HERE AS SUBJECTS-- NEVER AS ARTISTS.
THE WORLD HAS TURNED SMOOTHLY THROUGH THE AGES, WITH ONLY THE ART AND ARTISTRY OF MEN TO UPHOLD IT.
YOUR VOICES ARE UNNECESSARY.
SUCH A HARSH VIEW, THAT A SINGLE WORD FROM A WOMAN'S LIPS IS SO DISTASTEFUL AS TO KILL ALL LOVE.
NOT LOVE, MSSR.
ILLUSION.

THIS IS ALL LIE AND THEFT AND ILLUSION.
ACTIVE MEN AND PASSIVE WOMEN. EVEN YOUR QUEENS DO NOTHING BUT SIT--EVEN YOUR MONSTERS ARE MEANT, FIRST AND FOREMOST, TO ENTICE MEN.
YOU HAVE STOLEN OUR LIKENESSES, AND HAVE PUPPETED US TO SAY THE WORDS AND HOLD THE POSTURES YOU WISH TO SEE, AND CAL IT SUPERIOR TO WAKING LIFE.
YOU BAR US FROM SCHOOLS AND SHAME US FOR OUR IGNORANCE.
YOU BAR US FROM THE ARTS AND SAY NO GREAT WOMAN ARTIST EVER LIVED.
YOU COMPARE US TO WOMEN OF SILK TAPESTRIES AND STONE STATUES AND REVILE US OUR BLOOD AND SWEAT.
YOU NARRATE OUR LIVES, ROB OF THE PENS AND CANVAS TO TELL STORIES OF OUR OWN, AND THEN TELL US WHAT IT IS TO BE A WOMAN, AND WHAT A WOMAN SHOULD BE.
YOU CONTROL THE IMAGE AND THEN TELL US IT IS A REFLECTION.

I COULD SHOW YOU YOUR *REFLECTION*, IF YOU LIKE.
I KNOW MY REFLECTION WHEN I SEE IT.
WHEN YOU GO HUNTING IN THE STREETS FOR YOUR NEXT *MUSE*, MSSR, REMEMBER...
...*I* WILL BE *HUNTING*, TOO.
AND YOU WOULD TREMBLE AND WEEP AND PIERCE YOUR OWN EYES WITH YOUR PEN AT THE MERE *WHISPER* OF THE THINGS I CAN *INSPIRE*.
PHOEBE, SWEETEST.
LET US GO RELIEVE YOUR MOTHER OF DEAR WILL'S CARE.
MUSE, SHE CALLS HERSELF.
GO NOW.
BRING THEM AND THE OTHERS TO *THE BLACK ROOM*.
WE SHALL HAVE *NINE MUSES* FROM *THE SALON DE JARDIN VIOLET'S* FOUL HIVE.

Rue des Papillons Blancs. Home of Lady Bertram and Her Household.
"RODERICK AND HIS SQUIRMING LITTLE CULT TOOK THREE GRACES FOR THE THREE HE CLAIMS WE STOLE FROM HIM...
"...THE CURATOR OF THE MUSEUM IS MISSING...DO YOU THINK HE BELIEVES HIS ACTIONS ARE REVENGE FOR WHAT HE CLAIMS WE HAVE DONE?"
IF HE DOES, IT IS BUT AN EXCUSE.
HE HAS BEEN POACHING OUR PUPILS FOR WEEKS.
I SAW THE AD IN THE PAPER, READ WHAT WAS WRITTEN BETWEEN THE LINES.
I SOUGHT YOU OUT, MARIAH.
I THINK ANOTHER FORCE WORKS IN THE UNDERWORLD OF PARIS...
...BUT I DO NOT KNOW IF IT IS FRIEND OR FOE...
WHY DO THEY CALL YOU HARUSPEX, PHOEBE?
BOTH MSSR. RODERICK AND HIS SPIES HAVE NAMED YOU SUCH...

HEH. AH, MARIAH...
...THOUGH MY MOTHER RUNS HER OWN SECRET ACADEMIE, I AM LESS PAINTER THAN PROPHET, LESS SCULPTOR THAN SEER.
MY ART RUNS TO TAXIDERMIA.
I CAN TELL THE FUTURE IN THE INNER WORKINGS OF LIVING THINGS.
I READ OMENS IN THE SPILLED GUTS OF THE DEAD.
MY ART DOES NOT INFLUENCE LIFE.
LIFE INFLUENCES MY ART.
IN BLOOD.
IN BONE.
IN BODIES.

"I READ AND PAINT ALL EVIL THINGS TO COME."

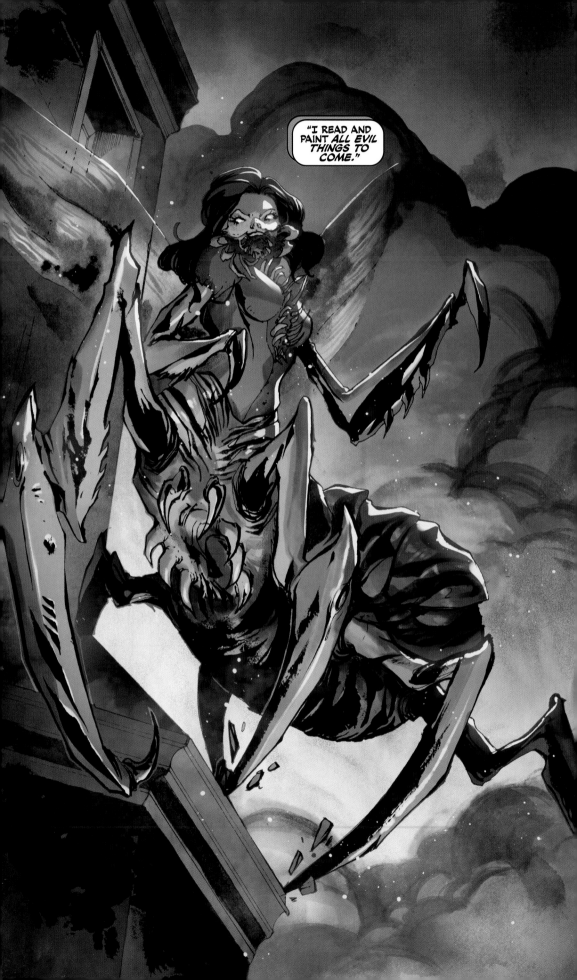

WOULD THAT I HAD SUCH PAINT AND EASEL *NOW.*
WILL THESE *SPIES* SUFFICE?
OH MY GOODNESS, LADY.
I AM BEGINNING TO UNDERSTAND THE *AFFECTION* MARIAH BEARS FOR YOU.
THE AFFECTION MARIAH BEARS, INDEED.

"WE ARE MAKING ART OF THE ARTISTS.

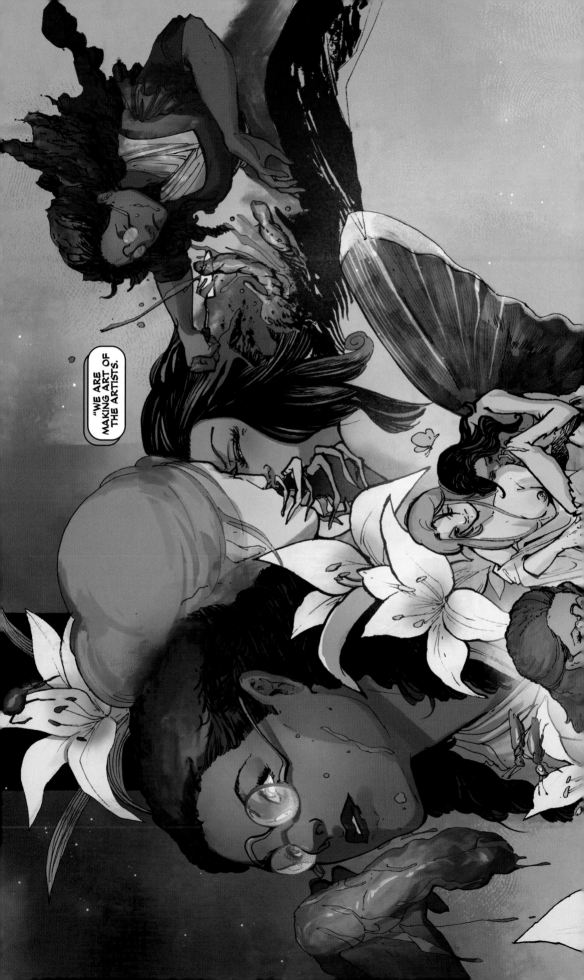

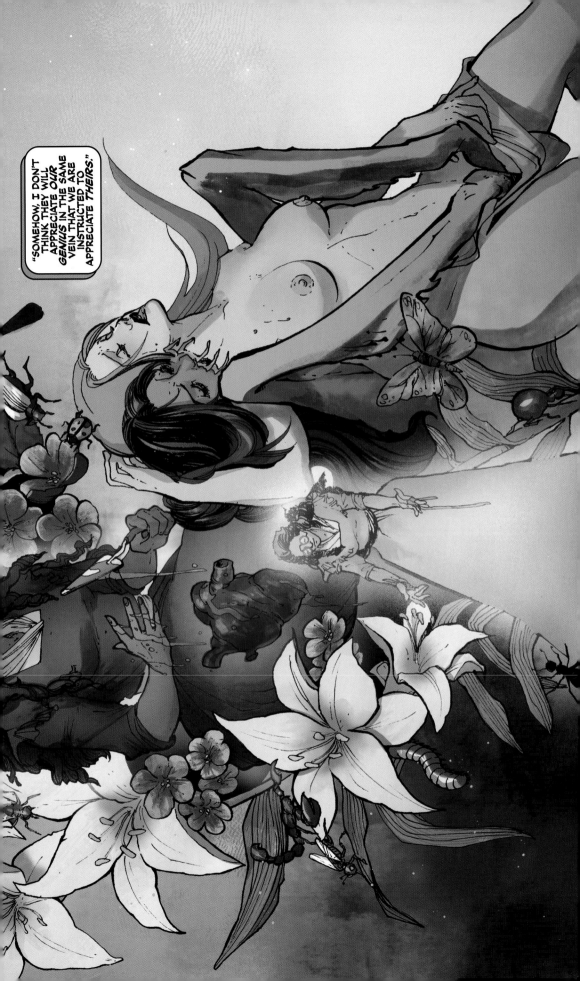

"SOMEHOW, I DON'T THINK THEY WILL APPRECIATE OUR GENIUS IN THE SAME VEIN THAT WE ARE INSTRUCTED TO APPRECIATE THEIRS."

I KNOW WHERE WE HAVE TO GO.
THE *NECROPOLIS* OF *SAINTE MARGUERITE D'ANTIOCHE*.

The Necropolis.
BLOOD, AND BONE, AND BODIES...
..."CITY OF THE DEAD"--THAT IS WHAT "NECROPOLIS" MEANS.
THE CITY OF BODIES, MUTE AND STILL, THE STORIES OF THEIR LIVES ENDED, OR WRITTEN OR REWRITTEN BY OTHERS, NOW.
I WAS A CHILD IN THE TIME OF AN GORTA BEAG, AND MY SISTERS TOLD ME TALES OF THE GREAT FAMINE ONLY A GENERATION PAST.
DEAD BODIES HOLD NO HORROR FOR ME NOW.
LIVING BODIES DO.
SOMETIMES, EVEN MY OWN.
THE HORROR OF BEING TRAPPED IN A VESSEL THAT DEFINES ME, CONSTRAINS ME, CHANGES UPON ME AND AGAINST MY WILL--
--A BODY WHICH IS ALL FOR WHICH I AM VALUED--
--A BODY THAT MUST BE GOVERNED AND CONTROLLED, TWISTED AND MAINTAINED, AND STILL IT CANNOT PROTECT ME FROM THE DESIRES OR RAGES OF OTHERS--
--THE COLOR OF ITS SKIN, THE NATION OF ITS BIRTH, THE HANDS OR HOLLOWS OR TONGUE WHICH CAN BE PUT TO USE OF THE WILL OF OTHERS!

WE WILL NOT BE REDUCED TO OUR BODIES.
THAT IS WHAT OUR ENEMIES SEEK.
THEY MEAN TO DEFINE US AS BODIES, OR THE IMAGES OF BODIES--OBLITERATE ALL SENSE OF PERSON AND PERSONHOOD.
WE ARE BODIES TO BE HANGED ON A WALL, BOUND TO AN ALTAR.
MY OWN MOTHER BORE A DAUGHTER, BUT UNTIL I HAD THE STRENGTH TO SPEAK, AND HAD BEEN TAUGHT THE WORDS TO NAME MYSELF...
...SHE MISBELIEVED THAT SHE HAD BORN A DIFFERENT KIND OF HEIR.
BUT THOSE WORDS WERE SO DIFFICULT AND DEAR, AND THE SEARCH WAS LONG AND BITTERSWEET...

...IF YOU ARE NEVER TO SEE YOURSELF DEPICTED...NOT IN STORY NOR SONG NOR POEM NOR PAINTING NOR PROSE...
...NO SHRED OF A TALE BY SOME DISTANT KINDRED SOUL WHO SAW AND KNEW AND FELT THEN AS YOU DO NOW, AND ELSE ANOTHER WHO LOVED AND BORE WITNESS...
...NEVER SEE YOURSELF EXCEPT AS CRUDE CARICATURE, MYTHICAL BEAST, OR MAGDALENE PENITENT...
...YOU BELIEVE NO OTHER LIKE YOU EVER EXISTED.
YOU BEGIN TO WONDER IF YOU EVEN EXIST AT ALL.
UNQUIET WOMEN, DEFIANT WOMEN--WE LIVE INVISIBLE LIVES, AND IF WE ARE SEEN AND SEEN BY STRANGERS, WE ARE REDUCED TO MONSTERS.
VAMPIRES, WHO HAVE NO REFLECTION IN A LOOKING GLASS.
MERMAIDS, WHO DIE AND BECOME SEA FOAM, BLOWN AWAY BY THE WIND.
WE WILL TAKE UP AND TAKE BACK THE TOOLS TO TELL OUR STORIES AS OUR OWN.
CIVILIZATIONS MAY RISE AND FALL AND REWRITE THE HISTORY OF THE DEAD, AS SO OFTEN THEY DO.
BUT WE WERE HERE...AND WE LIVED, AND LOVED, AND MATTERED.

AND OUR STORIES *WILL NOT DIE* WITH US, TO BE BURIED IN A NECROPOLIS OF ANGELS AND STONE.
"LOOK...*THE GRACES*...
"...THE *MISSING CURATOR*.
"AND THERE--?"

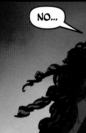

PT-PT-PT

"WHAT *ARE* THESE THINGS?

"AN ARMY...?

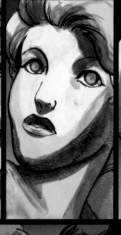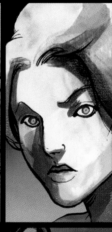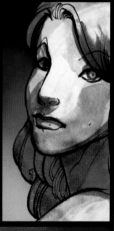

"A CULT...?"

NO...

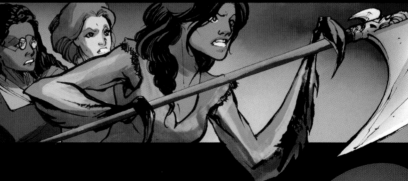

PT-PT HSSSSSSSS

...A GALLERY.
NEXT:
InSEXts
CHAPTER XI

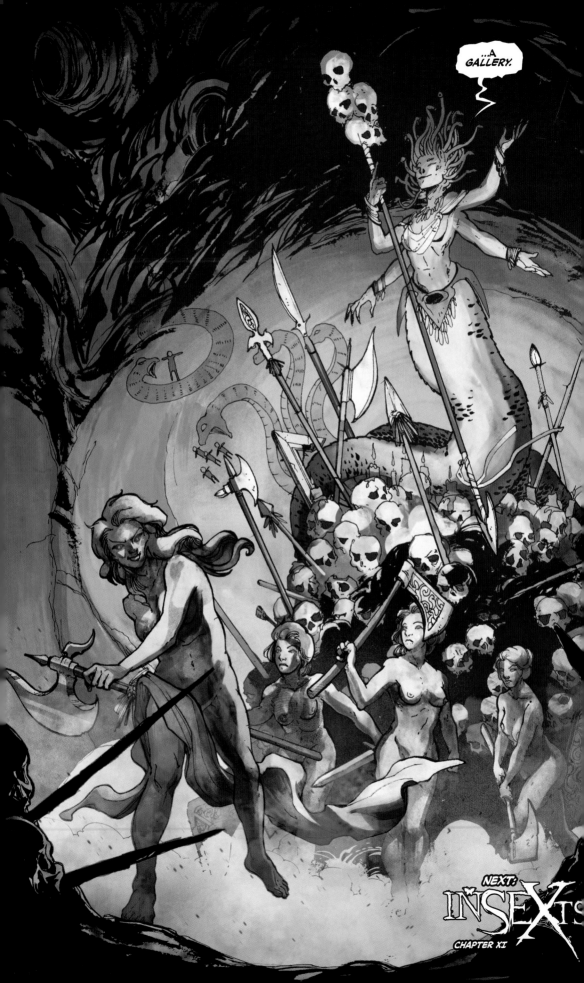

11

"THE MIRROR"

The Necropolis of Sainte Marguerite D'antioche.
Paris, 1897.
LONG HAVE I AWAITED THEE, SISTERS OF DEATH.
I SENT A GIFT WHEN I SENSED THEE HERE...
...A GRAVE ROBBER, MADE MONUMENT TO DECORATE THE GRAVES HE PILLAGED.
I SENSED THE BLOOD OF HIS MASTERS IN THE BONES OF THINE HOUSE.
THE MAN FROM THE MUSEUM WHO ATTACKED YOU, PHOEBE...
...WHO I USED IN THE RITUAL TO AWAKEN MY LADY.
AND I SEE THAT THOU HAST BROUGHT ME A GIFT IN KIND...
...ANOTHER SERVANT OF THE MEN WHO IMPRISONED ME.
PHOEBE IS OUR ALLY, ANCIENT QUEEN.
SHE IS NO SERVANT, LEAST OF ALL TO OUR ENEMIES.
IS THAT SO?

YOUR HIGHNESS...
...I WOULD STAKE MY AFTERLIFE ON IT!

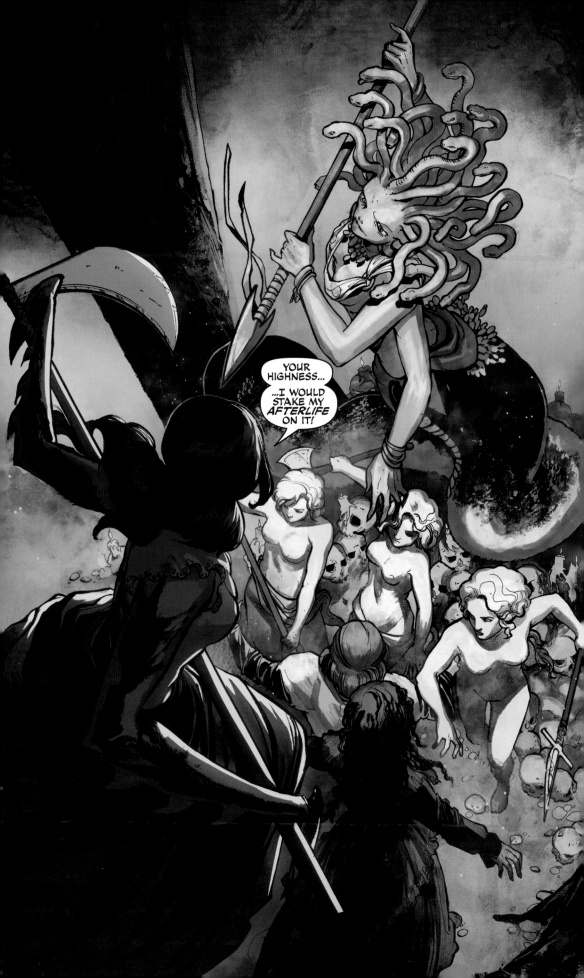

OH, THOU FRAGILE LITTLE MONSTER.
THOU ART NEW TO THE WORLD.
BUT I AM LEGEND.
LIFE AND DEATH, FLESH AND STONE, ARE ALL MINE TO COMMAND.
DO NOT PRESUME TO CHALLENGE ME.

MARIAH, *NO--!*
MY HEART ONLY KNOWS ONE *QUEEN,* O LEGEND--
--AND FOR *HARMING* HER, YOU SHALL--
N-NO!
I CONFESS!
YES, I ADMIT IT, I--
--I *SERVED* THE ONE WHO IMPRISONED YOU.
PLEASE-- *DO NOT HURT MY COMPANIONS!*
A YEAR AGO, I...
...I AIDED MSSR. RODERICK IN THE OPENING OF HIS MUSEUM.
BUT *NEVER* IN HIS *FIENDISH DESIGNS.*
HE CLAIMED IT WOULD BE A PLACE FOR WOMEN TO DISPLAY...
...HE ASKED MY AID IN *PROCURING ARTIFACTS* FOR HIM.
MY ART...MY ART RUNS TO *TAXIDERMIA.*

WAS ME.
I KNEW... I KNEW A GRAVE ROBBER.
A FOUL MAN WITH A FURIOUS TEMPER AND TEMPERED FISTS, BUT ONE WHO COULD KEEP A SECRET.
RODERICK... EMPLOYED THIS MAN TO SMUGGLE RELICS FROM CONQUERED LANDS.
ONE RELIC OF WHICH--
"BUT, OH, I AM NO RELIC. NO PARASITE. NO MONSTER.
"SWEET LITTLE GIRL-CHILD...
"...I AM A GOD.
"A GODDESS OF PROTECTION, FROM A DISTANT LAND.
"AND SOMETIMES...
"...A GODDESS OF REVENGE."

Island of Java.
1896.
"THEY TOOK ME FOR A *MEDUSA.*
"A STATUE OF THEIR *OWN PANTHEON.*
"*PILLAGED ART.*
"THE SPOILS OF *EMPIRE.*
"CARRIED ME AWAY LIKE A *SABINE WOMAN...*
"...BROUGHT THE *TROJAN HORSE* INTO THEIR CITY.
"I KILLED THE *GRAVE ROBBER* FIRST.
"THE ONE WHO BROUGHT ME TO THE DOCKS.
"*THE CURATOR* SECOND, WHO LAID HANDS UPON THE STONE OF MY SKIN AS I SLEPT.
"I HAVE HUNTED THE OTHERS, *ONE BY ONE...*
"...AND THOU HAST HELPED ME PUT THEM DOWN, FOR *THEY* ARE THINE ENEMIES, TOO."

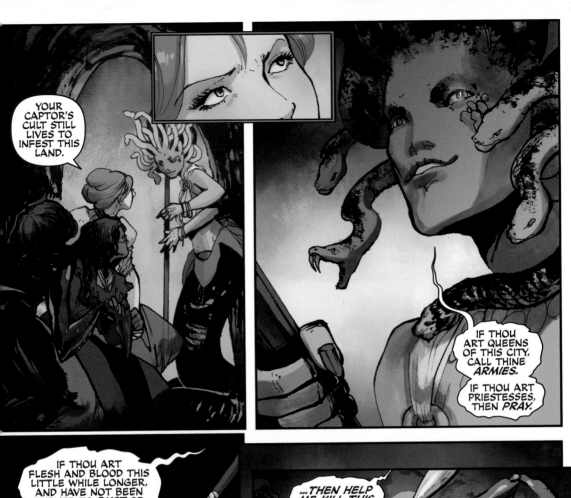

YOUR CAPTOR'S CULT STILL LIVES TO INFEST THIS LAND.

IF THOU ART QUEENS OF THIS CITY, CALL THINE *ARMIES*.

IF THOU ART PRIESTESSES, THEN *PRAY*.

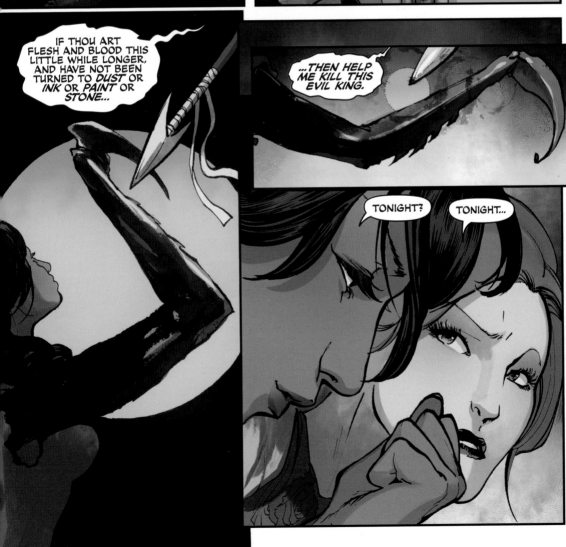

IF THOU ART FLESH AND BLOOD THIS LITTLE WHILE LONGER, AND HAVE NOT BEEN TURNED TO *DUST* OR *INK* OR *PAINT* OR *STONE*...

...THEN HELP ME KILL THIS EVIL KING.

TONIGHT?

TONIGHT...

Le Jardin Des Violets.
Salon and Studio of Mme. Dorothée de Azaïs.
"TONIGHT."
HELP ME WITH THE PAINTINGS, ANOUK.
MY DAUGHTER SENT WORD THAT WE MUST HAVE THEM IN READINESS.
OUR STOLEN GIRLS WILL BE BROUGHT HOME.
OUR LOST ARTISTS RESTORED.
AHH, NOT YET, LITTLE WILL.
YOUR MOTHERS WILL HELP US.
THEN WHAT NICE YOUNG LADIES YOU WILL HAVE THE CHANCE TO MEET.
BOOM BOOM BOOM
WHAT THE DEVIL--?

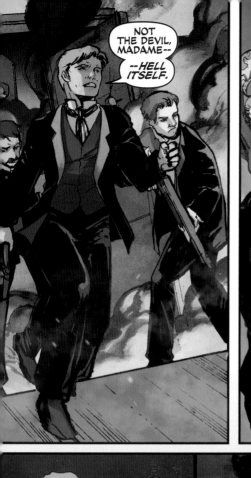

NOT THE DEVIL, MADAME--

--HELL ITSELF.

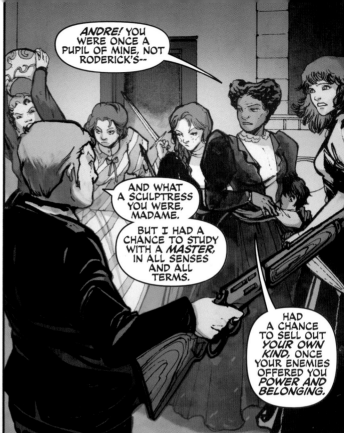

ANDRE! YOU WERE ONCE A PUPIL OF MINE, NOT RODERICK'S--

AND WHAT A SCULPTRESS YOU WERE, MADAME.

BUT I HAD A CHANCE TO STUDY WITH A MASTER, IN ALL SENSES AND ALL TERMS.

HAD A CHANCE TO SELL OUT YOUR OWN KIND, ONCE YOUR ENEMIES OFFERED YOU POWER AND BELONGING.

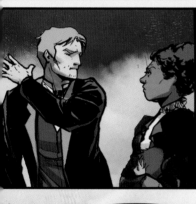

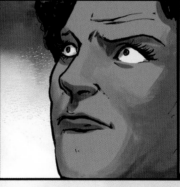

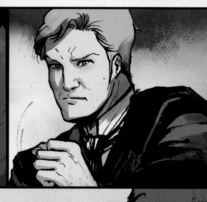

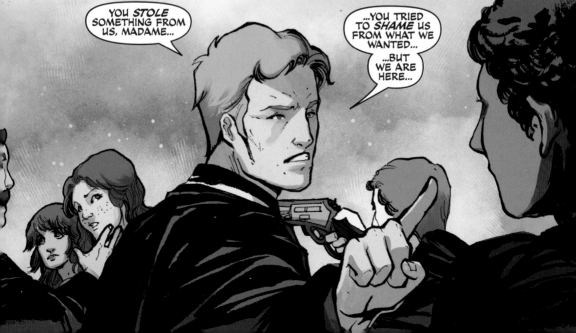

YOU STOLE SOMETHING FROM US, MADAME...

...YOU TRIED TO SHAME US FROM WHAT WE WANTED...

...BUT WE ARE HERE...

Le Musée Silencieux.
The Dark Room.
"...TO TAKE IT BACK."

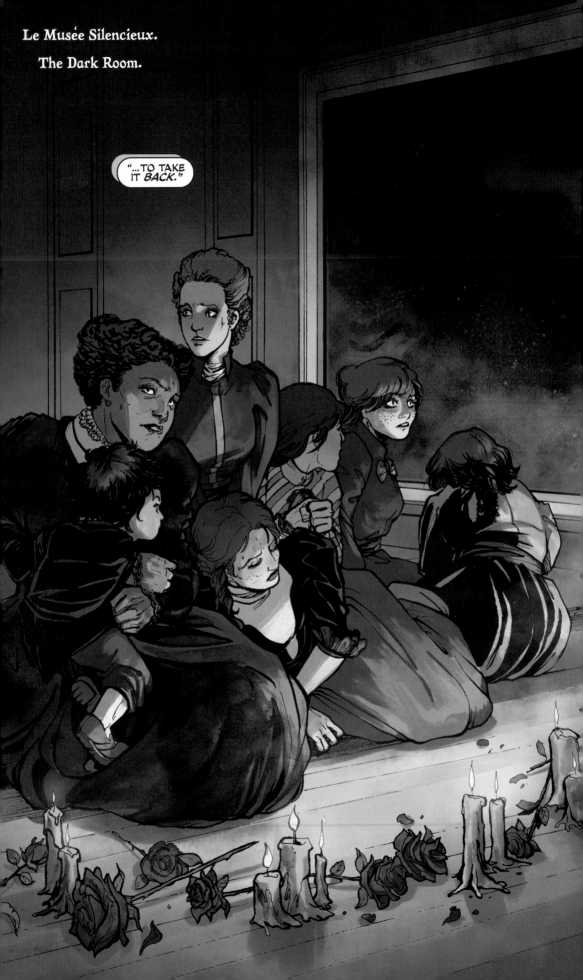

A PLEASURE YOU COULD JOIN US, MADAME DE AZAÏS.
R-RODERICK?!
WE HAVE *RECLAIMED* THE PAINTINGS YOU STOLE FROM US, FEATURING YOUR, AH, *"LOST" PUPILS...*
...AND TONIGHT, WE INTEND TO *ADD* TO THAT COLLECTION.
YOUR DAUGHTER AIDED US ONCE...
...AND HER INSOLENCE TODAY HAS AIDED US AGAIN...
...SHE AND HER TWO INDECENT COMPANIONS SHALL FINISH OUT OUR NEXT STATUES OF *THE NINE MUSES...*
...BUT YOU *SIX* SHALL BEGIN THEM.
WITH A *LITTLE EROS* THROWN IN, FOR *FUN.*
JUST THINK, MADAME...
...YOU WILL FINALLY HAVE SOMETHING TO CONTRIBUTE...
...TO *TRUE ART.*
SSSSSS

WILL--
--LOOK!

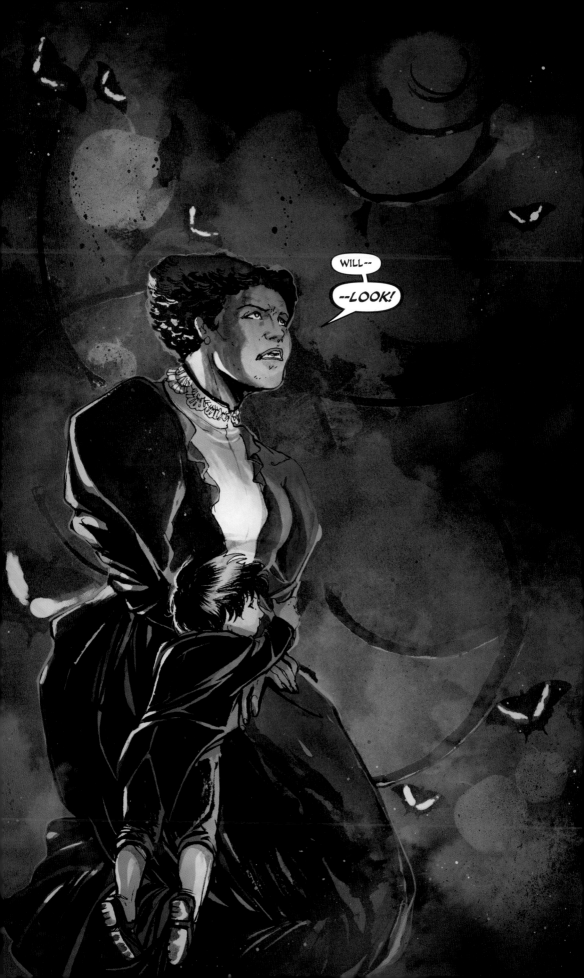

WHAT?! WHAT HAS HAPPENED IN THE DARK ROOM?!
THE MIRROR CANNOT WORK IN THE PRESENCE OF LIGHT!
WHAT IS THIS, WHO HAS SABOTAGED THIS--?!
WHO DO YOU THINK, MONSIEUR?
A MUSE.
SHHHLLTT

PHOEBE--
DAUGHTER!
MOTHER! GET THE STUDENTS AWAY FROM THE MIRROR!
RUN!

STOLEN RELIC FROM A LAND UNKNOWN...
...STOLEN AS *I* WAS STOLEN...
...DID THAT *GREEDY, SULLEN BOY* STEAL THEE AS WELL? DID HE SET THEE, TOO, TO WORK HIS FANTASIES?
SSSS...SSSS...
TWISTED THING...
...NO MORE SHALT THOU TWIST...
...UNBLINKING EYE...
...GAZE WITHIN THINE OWN ABYSS...
...THOU MISBEGOTTEN, HUNGRY THING...
...THOU NEVER WAST A *MIRROR*...

...THOU WAST A MAW.

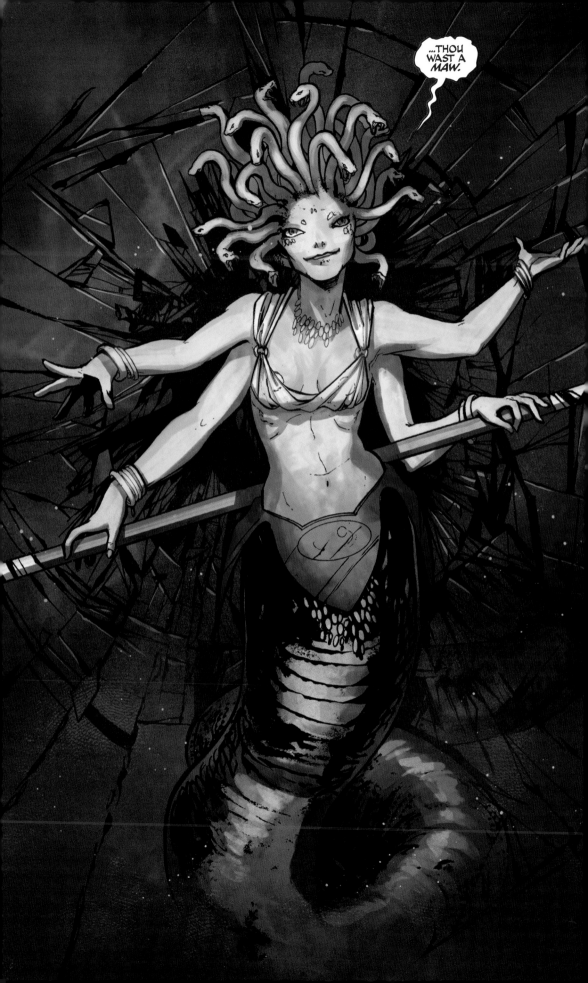

THE MIRROR! SHE HAS DESTROYED THE MIRROR!
?

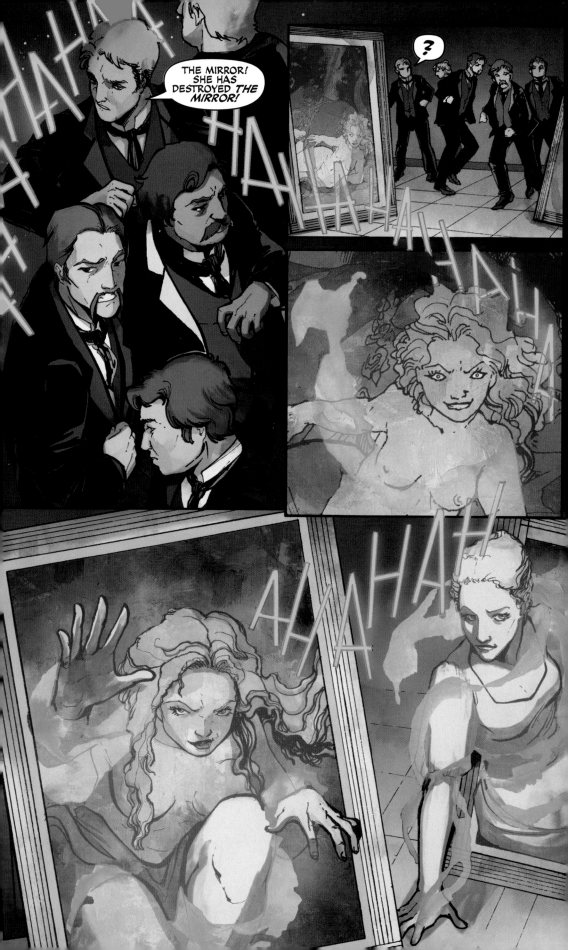

AHHH!
HAHAHAHAHAHA

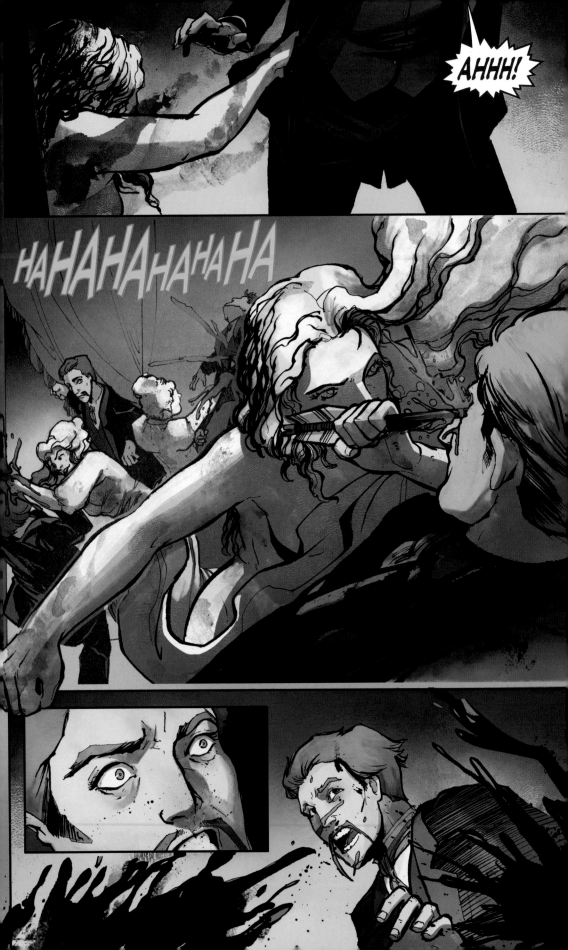

AAAAH!
?
YOU ASKED FOR MUSES--
--ARE YOU AMUSED?
YOU ASKED FOR GRACES, YET NEVER KNEW GRACE.
YOU MADE YOUR WISH, MONSIEUR, AND HERE WE ARE...
...YOUR FANTASY, MADE FLESH...

...YOUR DREAM, COME TRUE.
NEXT:
INSEXTS
CHAPTER XII

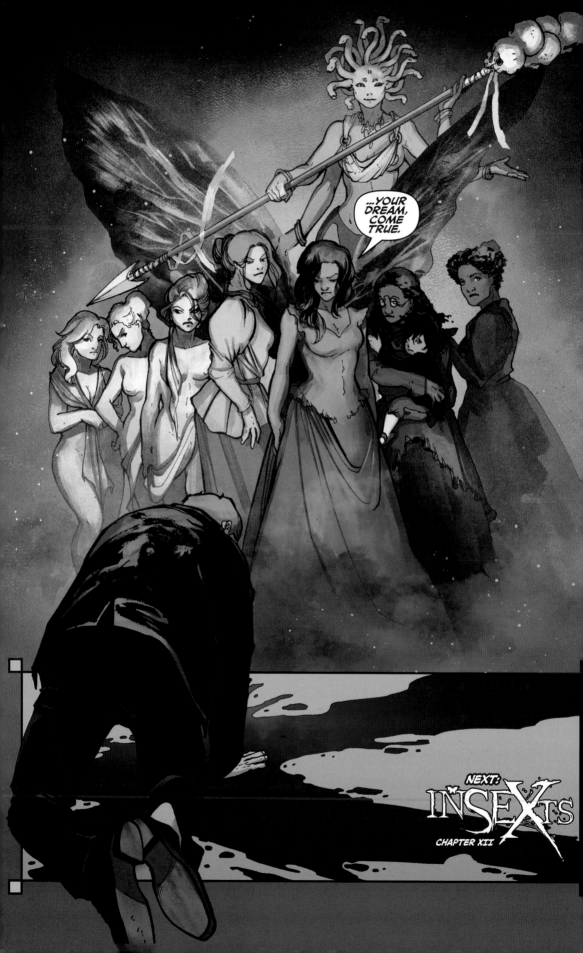

12

" UP ABOVE, DOWN BELOW"

Le Musée Silencieux.
Paris. 1897.
YOU WANTED MUSES.
YOU WANTED ART.
YOU WANTED WOMEN, STILL AND SILENT-- THE BLANK CANVASES ON WHICH YOUR FANTASY COULD BE BROUGHT TO LIFE.
EXOTIC AND ALLURING, OR MODEST AND PURE.
YOU TRIED TO MAKE THE PERFECT WOMAN.
BUT THERE IS NO PERFECT WOMAN.
THERE ARE ONLY WOMEN.
AND IF YOU STILL HELD THE BREATH OF GOD...

...YOU'D KNOW THAT IS POWERFUL ENOUGH.
ARE YOU FAMILIAR WITH A MAYPOLE, MONSIEUR?
MAIDENS DANCING, WEAVING RIBBONS, WRAPPING LONG AND SLOW AROUND THAT SHAFT OF SPRINGTIME.
ALL THE MANY MONSTERS WHO WOMEN BECAME...
...GORGONS, NOT GRACES.
WITCHES AND BITCHES AND BANSHEES...

MAIDENS LIKE MAENADS, WHO REVELED, WILD, IN THE WOODS.
MAIDENS TURNED MAENADS, WHEN THEY WOULD NOT DANCE UPON COMMAND.
WHOSE PARTIES GREW SO WILD, THEY KILLED THE STARRY-EYED DREAMERS WHO CROSSED THEIR PATHS.
...HAGS AND HARPIES AND WHORES.
SIRENS.
SUCCUBI.
FURIES.

FATES.

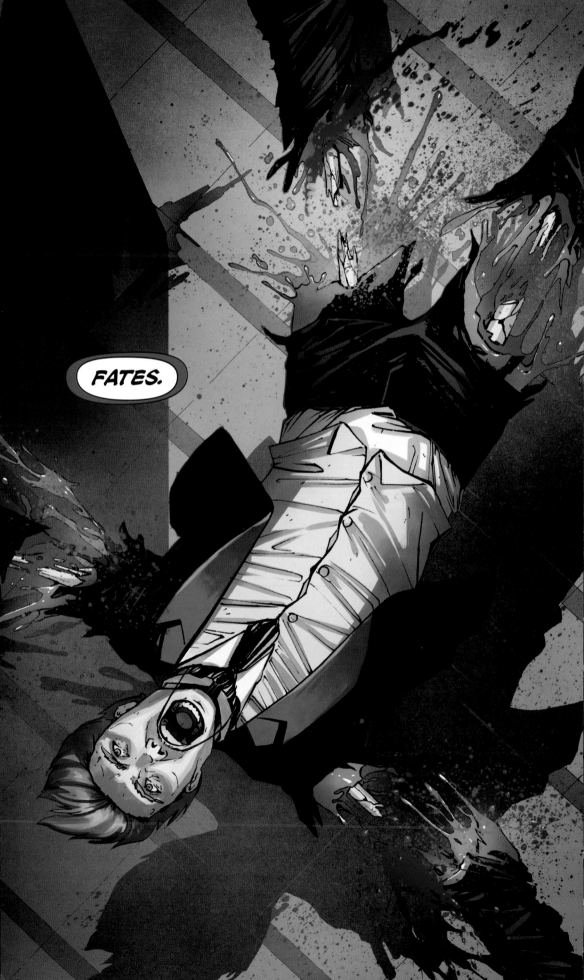

THE LOST WOMEN ARE RESTORED...
...THE FALSE EYE BLINDED, THE RAVENOUS MAW CLOSED.
THEIR CULT IS ENDED.
THEIR SERVANTS ARE SLAIN.
ALL BUT ONE...

...ALL BUT THEE, GIRL.
MY PHOEBE?! QUEEN, GODDESS-- SPARE HER!
MOTHER--?!
SHE SERVED THE ONES WHO TOOK ME PRISONER.
AND REPENTED THE ERROR!

PLEASE, MY QUEEN, DO NOT DO THIS--
THOU HAST FOUGHT ME ONCE, NEWBORN MONSTER...
...DOST THOU WISH TO KNOW DEFEAT AGAIN, SO SOON?
STONE--!
YOU NAMED ME GODDESS OF VENGEANCE...
...I HAVE ONE SOUL LEFT TO AVENGE...

"...MY OWN."

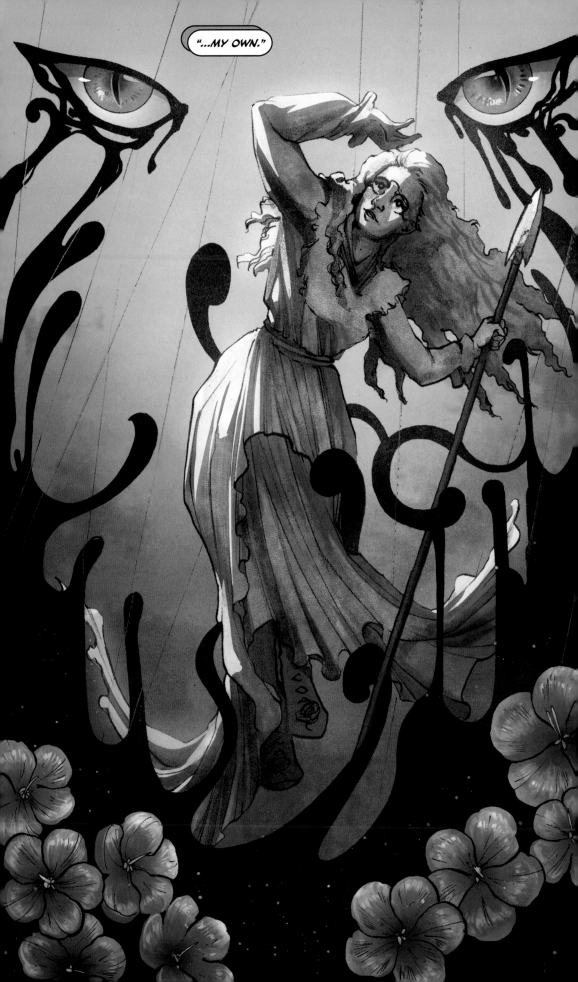

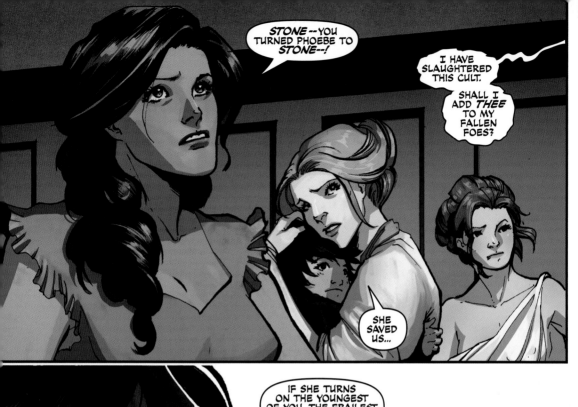

STONE--YOU TURNED PHOEBE TO STONE--!

I HAVE SLAUGHTERED THIS CULT.

SHALL I ADD *THEE* TO MY FALLEN FOES?

SHE SAVED US...

IF SHE TURNS ON THE YOUNGEST OF YOU, THE FRAILEST OF YOU, THE MOST VULNERABLE--

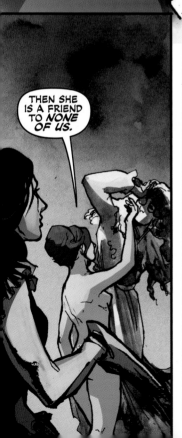

THEN SHE IS A FRIEND TO *NONE* OF US.

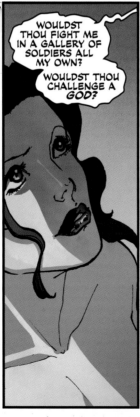

WOULDST THOU FIGHT ME IN A GALLERY OF SOLDIERS ALL MY OWN?

WOULDST THOU CHALLENGE A *GOD*?

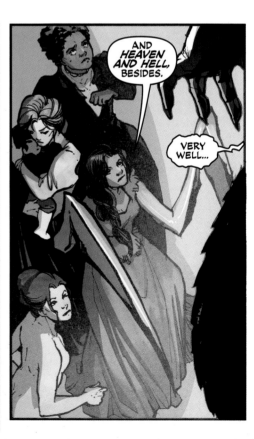

AND *HEAVEN AND HELL*, BESIDES.

VERY WELL...

...HEAVEN AND HELL *THOU SHALT HAVE.*

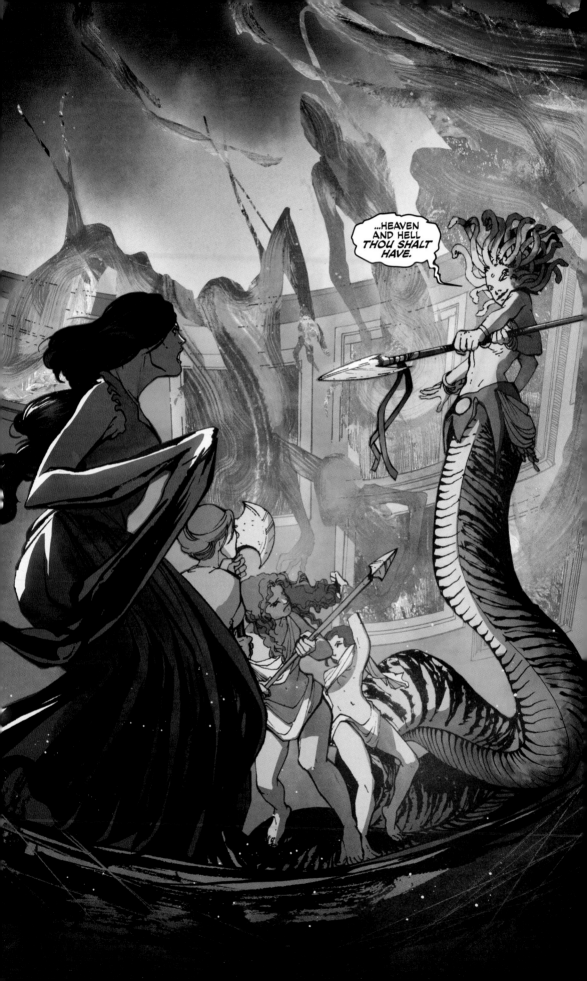

DOROTHÉE! GET MY SON TO SAFETY, PLEASE--
MY LADY--
DO YOU HAVE THE GIFT OF YOUR MOTHERS, WILL, THOSE OF WHICH PHOEBE SPOKE?
I NEED YOU TO FIND SOMETHING FOR ME, CHILD--
I WILL!
I SEE.
THERE--
RODERICK PROMISED MY DAUGHTER A PLACE IN THE MUSEUM, A PLACE TO DISPLAY...
...SHE BROUGHT HIM HER WORKS...

...SOLDIERS OF OUR OWN.

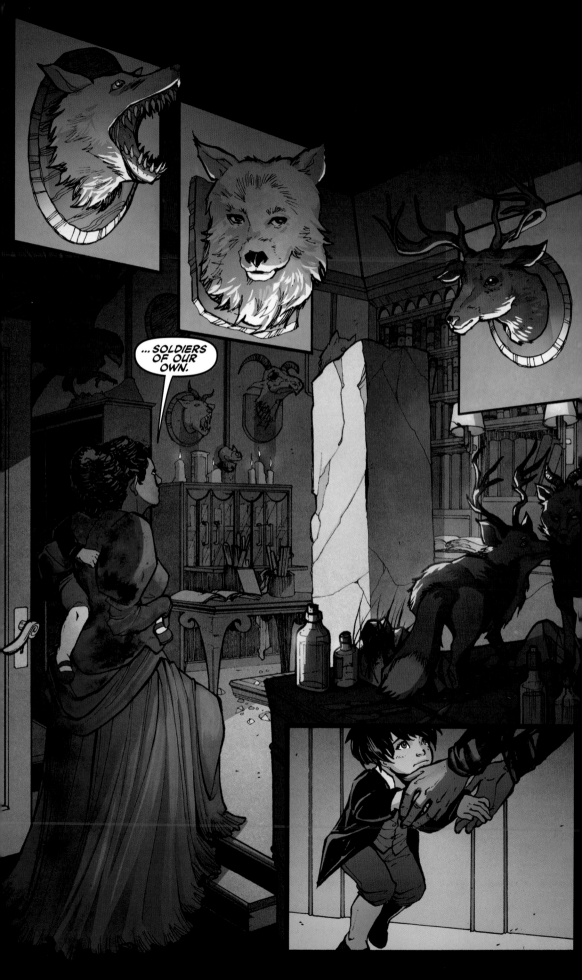

MADAME--WHAT ARE YOU DOING? HOW?
DOESN'T IT--DOESN'T IT TAKE WEEKS? DAYS, AT LEAST?
NOT FOR THIS.
PHOEBE KNOWS HER LITTLE MAGICS...
...AND SO DO I.
!
MADAME! SOMETHING IS WRONG--
--SOMETHING IS WRONG WITH YOUR LEGS--

NO...
...OH, MADAME...
...THEY ARE STONE!
YES, WILL.
BEGINNING WITH HER TOES...
...I KISSED HER TOES EVERY DAY, WHEN SHE WAS A BABY...WASHED HER, DRESSED HER, ADORED HER...
...HER LITTLE TOES.
WILL...
...YOU ARE LIVING PROOF THAT THERE IS NOTHING A MOTHER WILL NOT DO...
...FOR HER CHILD.

Up above.
"THIS GODDESS IS NOT TO BLAME.
"SHE WAS A PROTECTOR, ONCE, WITH LOVE AND CARE FOR HER KIND.
Down below.
"BUT SHE WAS PROFANED BY THE HATE SHE WAS GIVEN.
"BY THE HANDS THAT TURNED HER INTO THE MONSTER THEY CLAIMED SHE WAS.
"WE MUST FORGIVE TO THE EXTENT WE WOULD BE FORGIVEN.
"THOUGH WHAT KEEPS THE WORLD IN BALANCE HAS FAR TO DO WITH THE FORGIVENESS OF THOSE WHO WERE WRONGED--
"--THAN THE VIRTUE AND REMORSE OF THE REST."

"THE GODDESS THREW YOU INTO THE AETHER, MY DAUGHTER.
"THE PLACE WHERE ALL SOULS LIVE, BANISHED OR DEPARTED OR UNBORN.
"YOU SHALL BE *BEYOND* HER POWER.
"NOT BORN OF *FLESH.*

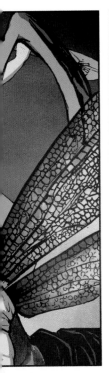
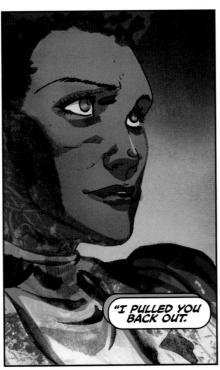
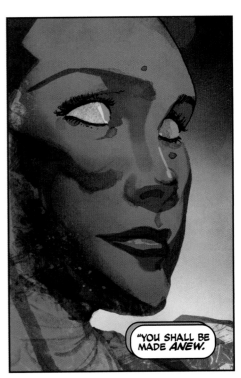

"I PULLED YOU BACK OUT.

"YOU SHALL BE MADE *ANEW.*

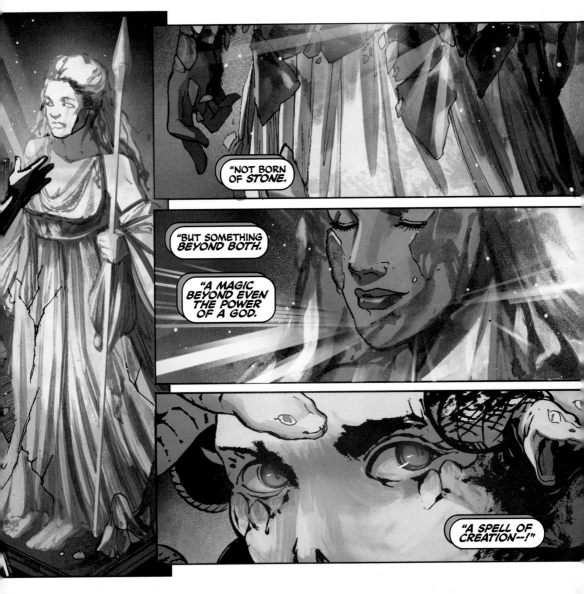

"NOT BORN OF *STONE.*

"BUT SOMETHING *BEYOND BOTH.*

"A MAGIC BEYOND THE POWER OF A GOD.

"A SPELL OF CREATION--!"

"TO POSSESS AND CREATE,
"AND BECOME...
"...YOURSELF."

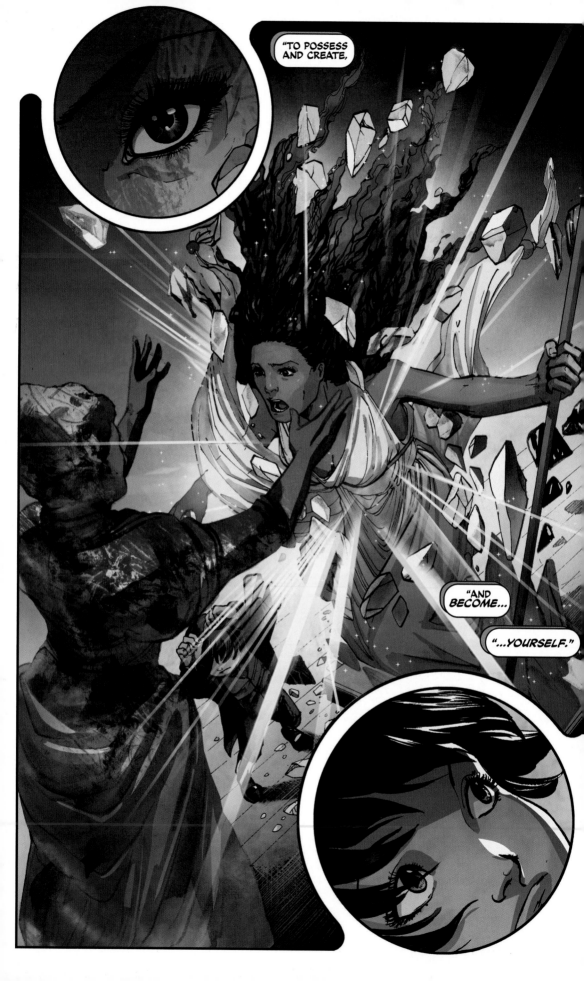

"TO LET NO ONE TAKE AWAY YOUR BODY--
"--YOUR WORDS--
"--YOUR IMAGE--
"--YOUR STORY--
"--YOUR SOUL."

"TO LET NO ONE...
"...TAKE YOU AWAY FROM YOURSELF...
"...EVER AGAIN."
NEXT:
INSEXTS
CHAPTER XIII

13

"VIOLENT ENDS"

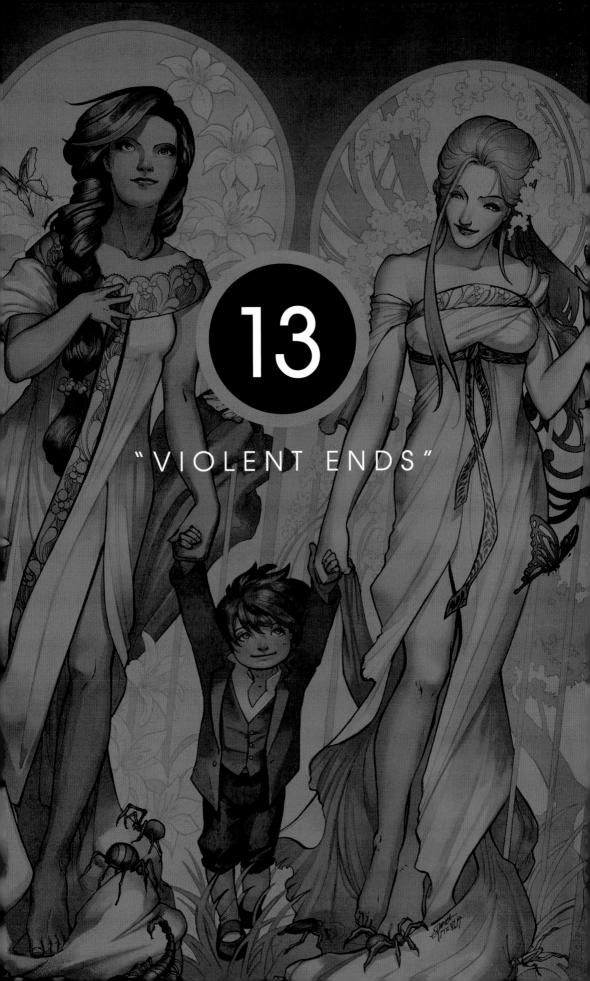

Le Musée Silencieux. Paris. 1897.
GODDESS, PLEASE, STOP!
WE NEED NOT BE ENEMIES, LITTLE REBELS--
YOU TOOK PHOEBE FROM US FOR A SIN LONG PAST PAID--
WE WILL NOT LEAVE ONE OF OUR OWN BEHIND!
VERY WELL.
IF THIS IS THE LAST WEAPON THOU DOST FEAR--
--THE FALSE MIRROR, THE CAGE--
--THE SILENCE WHERE THINE VOICES WOULD SING--

--THEN THIS IS THE WEAPON I SHALL BECOME!

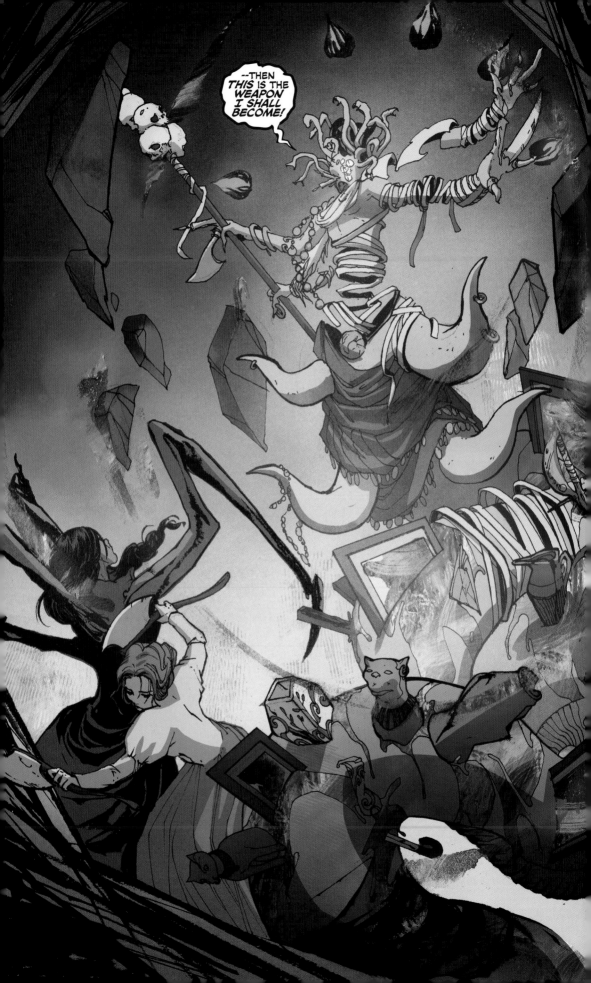

CRSSSSH
LADY!
THEY ARE NOT YOUR FOES, O GODDESS.
NOR AM I.
PHOEBE?!
HARUSPEX!
RBBBMMLL
I HAVE BEEN TO THE NECROPOLIS...

...AND I HAVE COME BACK.

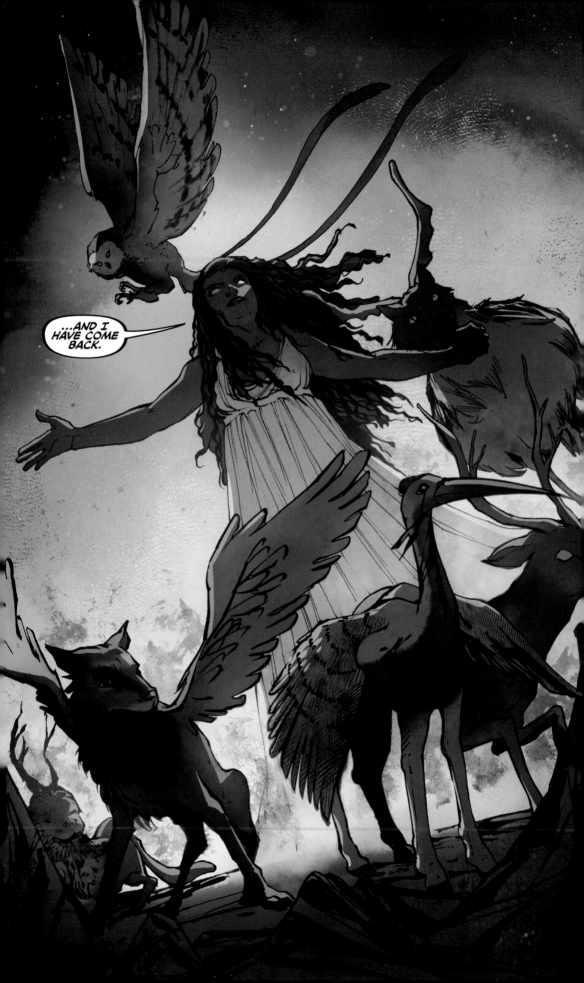

I HAVE CROSSED THE THRESHOLD.
MY CREATIONS ARE BEYOND LIFE AND DEATH, AND MADE NEW CREATURES.
THEY ARE REVENANTS, AND THEY ARE MINE.
THE DEAD WILL SPEAK AND TELL NEW TALES.
SACRIFICES WE WILL GIVE.
LIFE, AND DEATH, AND ART, AND STORIES...

...TO FREE YOU FROM THIS PRISON!
THE STORIES WE TELL MAKE THE WORLD THAT OUR CHILDREN ARE BORN INTO.

THE PICTURES WE PAINT MAKE THE WORLD INTO WHICH OUR *CHILDREN GROW.*
THIS IS *BENEATH* YOU, O GODDESS.
DO NOT BECOME THAT WHICH HAS HARMED YOU.
DO NOT CLOTHE YOURSELF IN THE LIE THEY WOULD HAVE YOU WEAR.
THEY WOULD MAKE YOU THINK YOURSELF A *MONSTER...*

...BUT YOU ARE SO MUCH MORE.

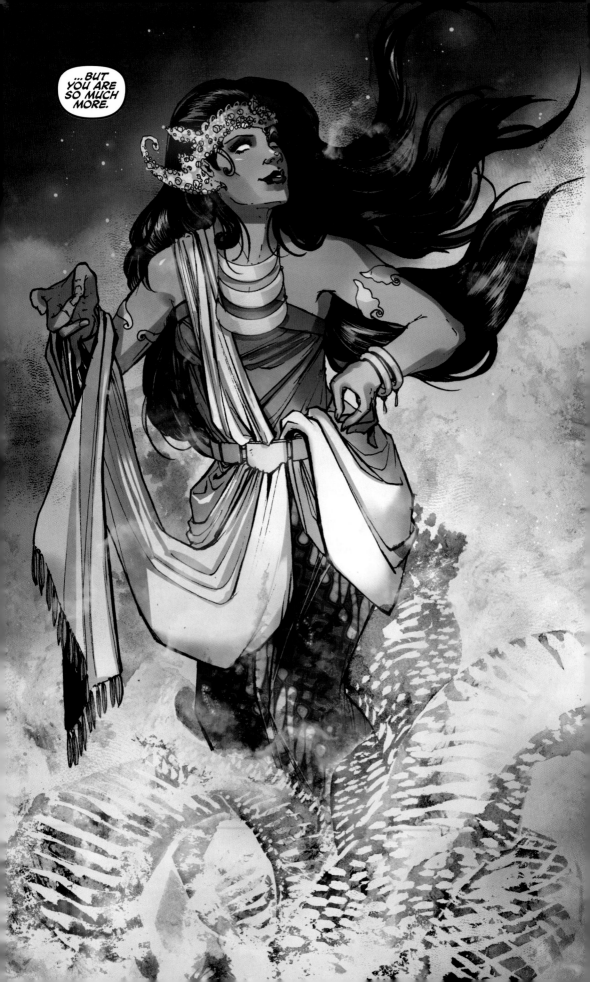

OUR LIVES ARE OUR STORIES, ARE THEY NOT?

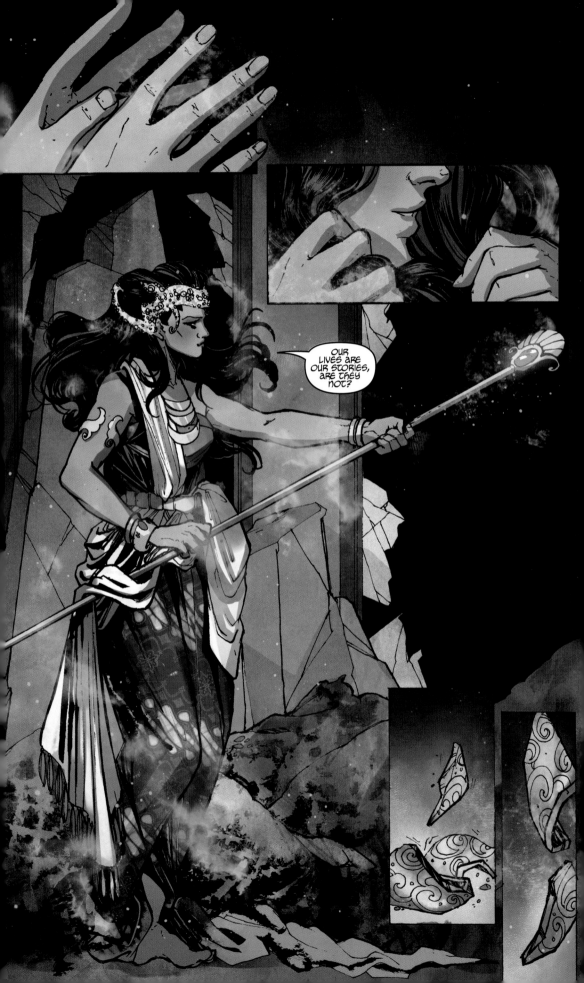

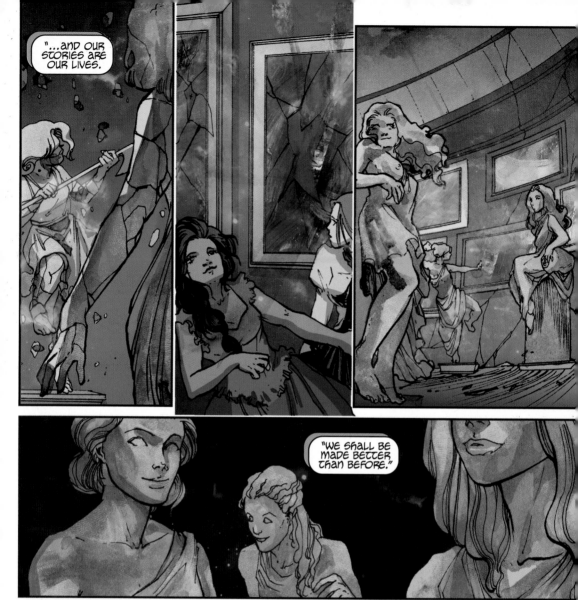

"...AND OUR STORIES ARE OUR LIVES.

"WE SHALL BE MADE BETTER THAN BEFORE."

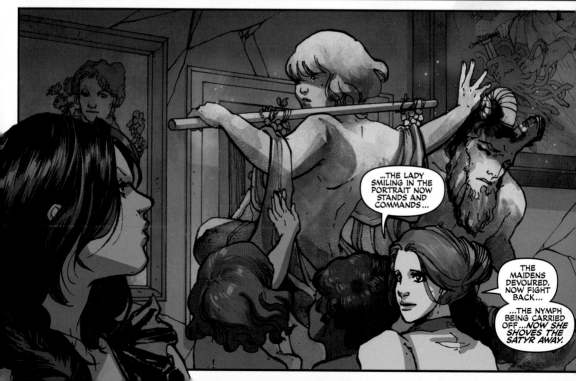

...THE LADY SMILING IN THE PORTRAIT NOW STANDS AND COMMANDS...

THE MAIDENS DEVOURED, NOW FIGHT BACK...

...THE NYMPH BEING CARRIED OFF...NOW SHE SHOVES THE SATYR AWAY.

PHOEBE'S MOTHER, DOROTHÉE...
ONE MORE, MADAME...
MOTHER MOST LOVING, MOST DEVOTED...
...YOU WHO GAVE YOUR LIFE, BODY AND SOUL TO RESTORE YOUR CHILD TO HERSELF...
...YOU WHO CREATED LIFE, NOT ONLY IN FLESH AND BLOOD, BUT IN THE TEACHING OF THE POWER BY WHICH OTHERS MIGHT TELL STORIES OF THEIR OWN...

...awaken...

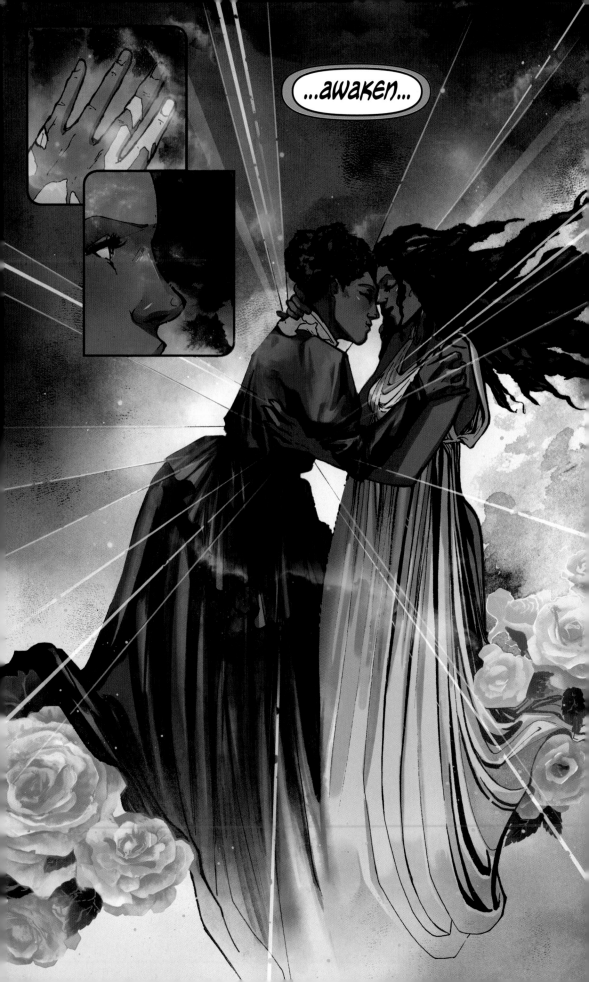

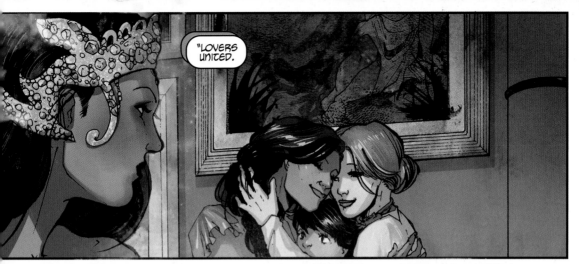

"LOVERS UNITED.

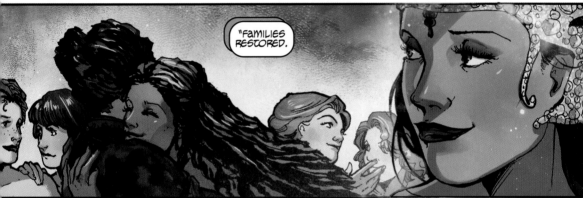

"FAMILIES RESTORED.

"THE WOUNDED AVENGED.

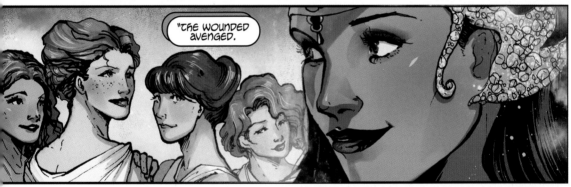

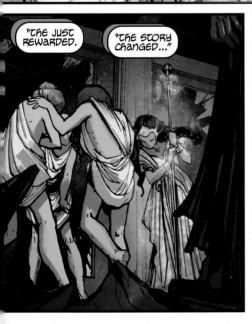

"THE JUST REWARDED.

"THE STORY CHANGED..."

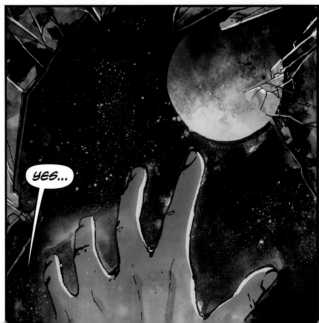

YES...

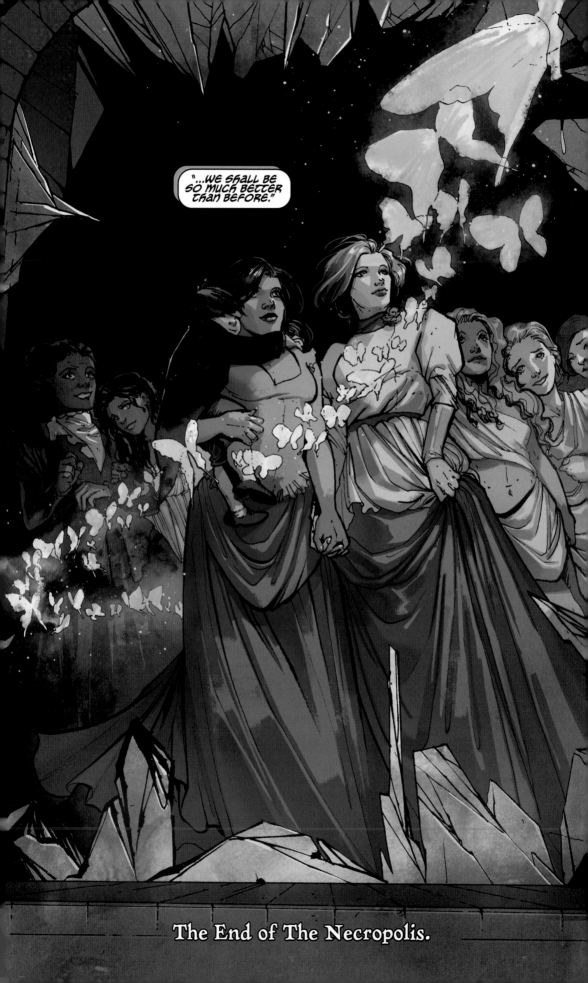

The End of The Necropolis.

pilogue.
ort of La Rochelle, Paris.
Noon.
LAST CALL, LADIES AND GENTLEMEN, FOR PASSAGE ABOARD *THE SPHINX* TO *NEW YORK CITY!*
MY HALF-SISTER SAYS EVERYTHING IS IN READINESS, MARIAH, AND THAT SHE IS MORE THAN HAPPY TO TAKE US IN.
POOR DEVIANT OUTCASTS THAT WE ARE.
"RICH WIDOWS MUST BE MARRIED, BURIED, OR SHUT UP IN A CONVENT," THE SAYING GOES.
HALLO, LADIES, CKETS PLEASE, TICKETS, AND ONE FROM THE LITTLE LAD--
--STEP RIGHT P, AND A SAFE JOURNEY, LADY--
FIRST DECK ROOM C
AND YOU, YOUNG MAN? *TICKET,* PLEASE?
EUGH, HAVE YOU BEEN *DRINKING,* SON?

The Deck of The Sphinx.
Sunset.

--NOTORIOUS *LADY BERTRAM* ABOARD, THEY SAY SHE'S *RICH AS CROESUS*--

--AND SHE'LL COME TO *NO* BETTER AN END--

CLIK

?

AND PHOEBE TOLD ME THEY WILL ALL BE WELL-ESTABLISHED IN MILAN...

!!

"...SALONS OF SORCERY, COVENS AND COTERIES..."
...AND THERE IS NEWS THAT THE GODDESS HAS RETURNED TO HER SHRINE IN BATAVIA, ARIENNE HAS SENT WORD...
CLIK
...DUTCH SOLDIERS DESERTING THE ISLAND...
BEDTIME, LITTLE WILL.
THINK OF ALL THE FUN YOU'LL HAVE WITH YOUR AUNTIE AND COUSINS IN NEW YORK CITY--
"--A KINGDOM WE WILL BUILD YOU, ALL YOUR OWN."
H, HANDS FF! THAT MY DUTY, MY LADY.
DUTY, INDEED?
DUTY...

HEH, HEH...
WAIT, MY LOVE...
...I SCENT SOMETHING.
AND PLEASURE.
I CAN SEE IT IN THE AIR...
...A TRESPASSER...
...WITH PRYING EYES.
OH, DID YOU THINK WE WERE FOR YOU?
DID YOU THINK WE WERE FOR YOUR PLEASURE? ALL FOR YOUR ENJOYMENT?
HERE, THE COMB IN MY HAIR, MY LADY, IT'S SHARP AS A HATPIN...
N-NO--!
TELL ME-- DID YOU THINK THAT WHAT IS OURS WAS YOURS TO TAKE?
OH, SIR...

...YOU WERE WRONG.
THE END

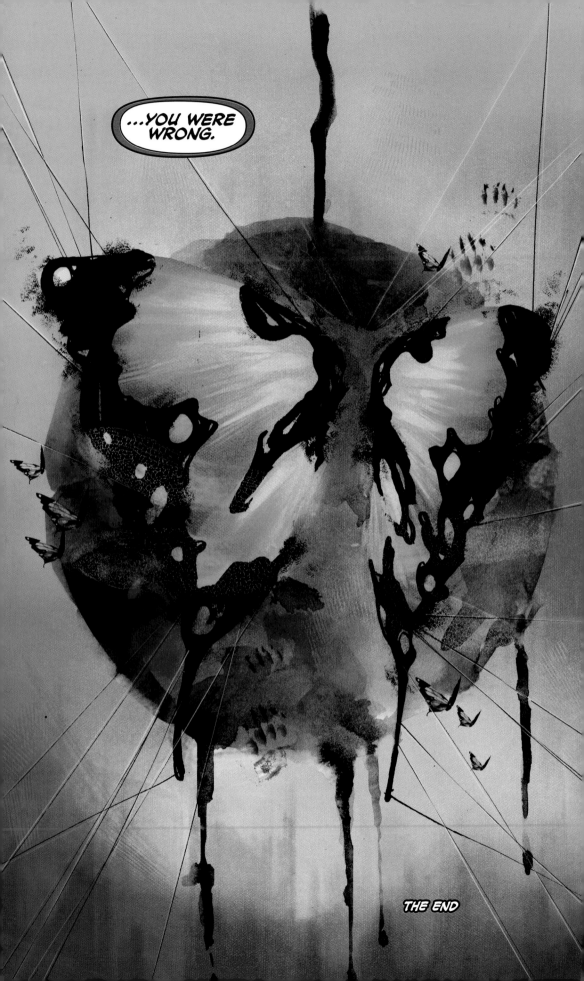

issue 8
NYCC variant cover
ELIZABETH TORQUE

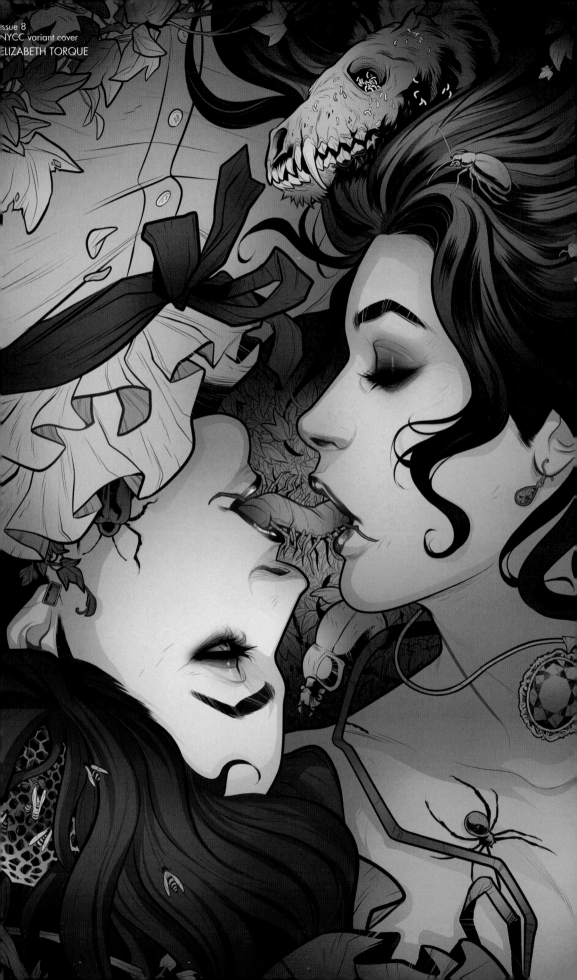

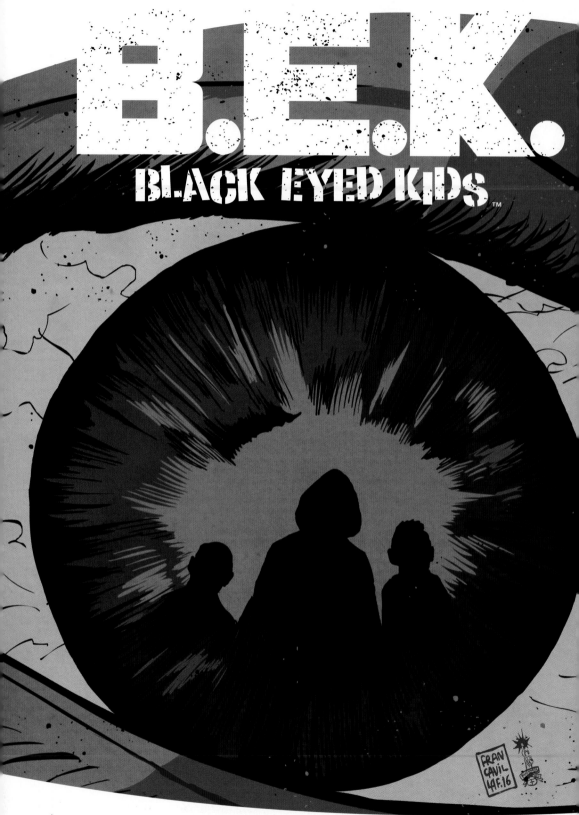

They say that EYES are the windows to the SOUL...

JOE PRUETT   SZYMON KUDRANSKI

B.E.K.
BLACK EYED KIDS ™

**RESERVE THIS
AFTERSHOCK SERIES TODAY!**

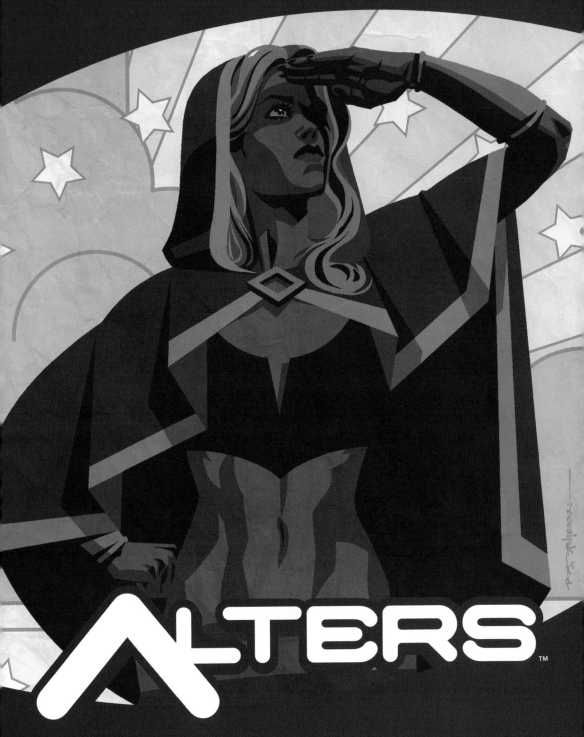

The saga of a young woman who can only really be herself...whenever she is not herself.

ALTERS™

CREATED AND WRITTEN BY
PAUL JENKINS
(WOLVERINE: ORIGIN, SENTRY, HELLBLAZER)
WITH ART BY LEILA LEIZ

ON SALE NOW!

MISSED AN ISSUE?
EXCLUSIVE COMICS & DIE-CAST PINS!
BACKLIST COMICS & COLLECTIONS!
AFTERSHOCK eSTORE
NOW OPEN!
aftershockcomics.com/store
GRADED & SIGNED COMICS!
#5
ROUGH RIDERS
9.8
White
CBCS Certified Comic
Insexts #2
MARGUERITE BENNETT · ARIELA KRISTANTI
INSEXTS
+ MORE!

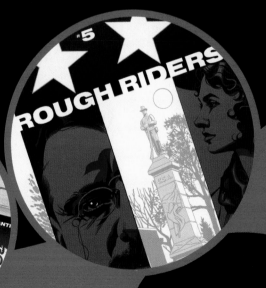

AFTERSHOCK

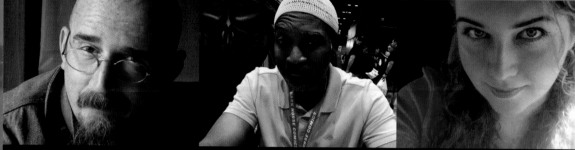

WE HAVE TOP WRITERS AND TOP ARTISTS

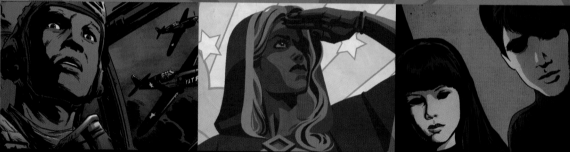

WE HAVE DIVERSE CHARACTERS AND WORLDS

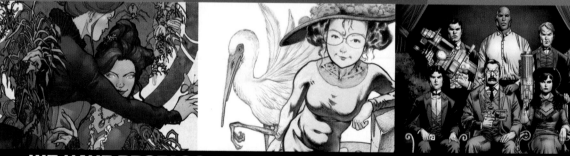

WE HAVE PROTAGONISTS OF ALL GENDERS AND SPECIES

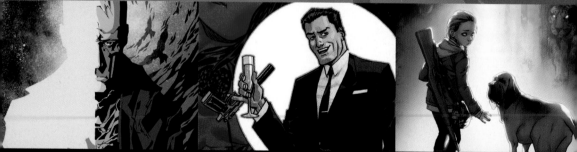

WE HAVE SELF-CONTAINED, EASY TO PICK-UP STORIES

WE HAVE THE COMICS YOU'RE LOOKING FOR

AFTERSHOCKCOMICS.COM